chasing moonlight

ANN ELIZABETH STEWART

Order this book online at www.trafford.com/08-1127
or email orders@trafford.com

Most Trafford titles are also available at major online book retailers.

Note for Librarians: A cataloguing record for this book is available from Library and Archives Canada at www.collectionscanada.ca/amicus/index-e.html

ISBN: 978-1-4251-8628-9

We at Trafford believe that it is the responsibility of us all, as both individuals and corporations, to make choices that are environmentally and socially sound. You, in turn, are supporting this responsible conduct each time you purchase a Trafford book, or make use of our publishing services. To find out how you are helping, please visit www.trafford.com/responsiblepublishing.html

Our mission is to efficiently provide the world's finest, most comprehensive book publishing service, enabling every author to experience success. To find out how to publish your book, your way, and have it available worldwide, visit us online at www.trafford.com/10510

www.trafford.com

North America & international
toll-free: 1 888 232 4444 (USA & Canada)
phone: 250 383 6864 • fax: 250 383 6804 • email: info@trafford.com

The United Kingdom & Europe
phone: +44 (0)1865 487 395 • local rate: 0845 230 9601
facsimile: +44 (0)1865 481 507 • email: info.uk@trafford.com

10 9 8 7 6 5 4 3

This book is dedicated to Tony for his unfailing encouragement and to my mother for her eternal nurturing.
Thank you both.

About the Author

ANN STEWART lives in the leafy Hill's district of Sydney with her husband, two dogs and occasionally her adult son and daughter. She has a degree in Education with majors in History and English literature and a semester of Law that persuaded her to take up knitting. She has decades of writing experience specialising in grocery lists and sick-notes and this is her debut novel. She wishes to assure her readers that all the characters are fictional but if they wish to appear in her next novel all bribes and inducements will be scrupulously considered.

She raced up the stairs to the church entrance and paused as she tried to quieten her racing heart. There were massed displays of white lilies and roses overflowing from the vases adorning the altar and the candlelight was throwing shadows onto the stained glass windows and competing for dominance with the late afternoon sun filtering through them.

She hesitantly started the walk down the aisle questioning again if she was making the right decision. She raised her eyes to the altar and saw him. "Please turn," she begged and he turned his head as if in answer to her unvoiced prayer. He saw her and an eye-creasing smile lit his face. The smile breathed life into his face and her doubts began to melt.

1

SHE LIED. They all lied—the beauty therapists, the magazines stacked in front of me, my hairdresser.

"This will make you feel better," she said as she applied the last of the foiled highlights to my newly-cut hair.

I checked my reflection in the bright lights of the salon mirror and met her proffered smile with my own. It was amazing how convincing my smile looked—a triumph of photo-shopping skill honed to perfection in tedious years of design work. I lowered my eyes to the open book in my lap in the desperate hope of deflecting further conversation.

"Wow! That will certainly while away a few hours ... You're lucky you have time to read. I'm always too busy," she said in the self-satisfied way adopted by those who believe in their own morally superiority. She set the timer for twenty minutes, placed it beside the obligatory cappuccino and wandered off to a chattier client.

I watched the minutes tick loudly away and wondered if she was right and busyness was a virtue—would frenetic activity really keep time at bay? Would it cease to be a capricious giver granting me too many minutes yet not enough days, if I just kept busy?

There were too many unfilled hours—too much time to think or read. My brain however had become sluggish and could not handle anything too taxing so I had been working my way through the chic lit novels that had hit the shelves of my local bookstore. I had devoured everything from Bridget Jones' Diary to all the latest offerings from the Irish writers with a small serving of the American genre for some balance. If there was Australian chic lit I had yet to find it.

The lives of the twenty and thirty-somethings had started to bore me so I had opted for something different. This book that was beckoning now promised that there was humour to be found even in menopause—four hundred pages of it in fact. Not that the country of origin or even the age of the protagonist affected the story-line—the premise was always the same.

It was always a Cinderella tale—the woman, a little downtrodden but with a great sense of humour is devoted to her husband and children until left by her husband for a younger woman. She is devastated, has a breakdown but then discovers exercise, a healthy lifestyle and a new assertiveness.

She finds a new man and more often than not a great new fulfilling job as well where her talents are finally recognised. Her ex-husband is also quite attracted to the newly assertive streamlined woman he previously rejected. This is often attributed to blonde highlights and the compulsory life-altering haircut.

These stories had provided me with a chuckle on occasions and I cheered on the heroines in their quest for smaller thighs and true love the second time round.

It had not taken me long to see the similarity between my life and that of the chic- lit heroines—for my husband too was about to leave me.

I was surrounded by people telling me to say goodbye and let him go. It was just part of the cycle of life, they told me. It was beyond my control—losing weight, getting blonde highlights would not change a thing. Crying, telling him how much I loved him, the fact I felt my life was ending—none of this mattered. The fact that we had been together for over twenty years and produced three beautiful children—none of this mattered. The fact that we had clung to one another desperately when we buried one child at four months—even this could not hold him.

He told me that our children would be fine. The twins would cope. They are adults now and had their own lives to lead. I too would be fine, he reassured. I was strong, he said, my life would go on. I did not have to worry about money; it was all taken care of. I might want to move into a smaller house, he suggested; that is, if I didn't wish to continue living in the house we had designed and shared for most of our married lives. But he was not trying to rush me; I could do it when the time felt right to me; he just wanted me to be happy without him.

I begged. I ranted. Logic deserted me. I became obsessed by the thought that I would no longer be able to tick the married category on surveys and travel documents. But none of this changed a thing—my husband was still going to leave me.

My husband was still going to die.

The advertising campaigns of the nineties had told us that cancer was a word not a sentence. They were partly right. It started as just a word—a word that described blurred vision, headaches and fatigue. It soon became a sentence though, the very worst sentence.

'Your husband has an inoperable brain tumour,' sort of made any other sentence pale into insignificance. The sentence is always punctuated by a full stop and that was what I was waiting for now; not just a metaphor anymore but the real thing, the genuine full stop, the last breath.

I didn't handle it well. I couldn't calmly say goodbye and tell him it was alright to go. It wasn't alright. I hated him for leaving me. He should have fought harder, we should have married younger. We should have met in preschool so we could have had more time together. I was selfish. I wanted him here to help me with my grief the way he had when our baby died. I helped him when his mother died. He helped me when my father died. It was all part of the deal, the quid pro quo of loving. But now he was not living up to his part of the bargain.

He had left me. The bastard.

Of course everybody else thought that I was coping beautifully.

The nursing staff had not seen my outbursts. They believed I was stoic. I knew I was numb.

Everybody said the funeral was beautiful, non-religious, with a new-age feel; just what he wanted.

Everybody said I was a tower of strength for the children; how well I kept their lives stable so that they could continue with their education.

Everybody said I was fortunate that Steve had left us well off financially. His foresight in taking out adequate life and sickness and accident policies, they told me, was a sign of his love for me.

Everybody kept telling me that I looked good. The exercise that I had kept up through his illness as my only stress relief had kept me fit and the weight that I had lost because all food now tasted like ash apparently suited me, or so they said.

I was becoming heartily sick of what everybody said.

My life seemed to embrace the chic-lit doctrine of career crisis also. My employer had been understanding when Steve was first diagnosed but I had soon used up all of my sick and annual leave entitlements. After six months leave-without- pay they realised they could do without me and I realised that I never really liked the job anyway.

The fashion industry, not surprisingly is a shallow industry. I had started out full of enthusiasm as part of the design team but with so much time off had been forced to fill in at the administrative level.

Call me fickle but I no longer felt outraged that the new hibiscus print was ruined because the petals looked more candy pink than fuchsia. I could no longer feign the enthusiasm to offer an opinion on whether this season's new black should be gunmetal grey or steel grey. I no longer had the patience to explain to customers that it was not a conspiracy against them personally that their size in this season's *must have* item was sold out nor to explain that, yes, sold out meant just that and, no, I did not have a supply secreted away for myself or some vacuous celebrity.

Death is a real downer, it takes all the fun out of fashion.

Still, here I was widowed, still attractive apparently and on the right side of forty-four. My beautiful gorgeous twins were now twenty-one, finished university and ready to embark on their lives free from guilt and worry about their mother.

Rebecca and Josh were alike yet very different. Striking thickly lashed midnight blue eyes graced both faces and they shared creative flair and musical ability. Their mutual love of music fed their closeness and supported them through many tough times. It was not unusual to see them sharing a headset to listen to some new artist one of them had discovered or a new track Josh had written and on which he nervously wanted feedback.

Rebecca however was honey blonde with only slight assistance from a good hairdresser. She was tall and slim but curvy with fine ankles, shapely legs and full breasts. She was lightly tanned with a sprinkling of freckles and a fierce intelligence and was about to embark on a year as an exchange student at a New York fine arts college. She had been designing and selling her own jewellery for years but her new passion was sculpture and she was keen to develop her skills in an international setting.

Josh was as dark as Rebecca was fair. He was a little over six feet and lean and fit. His skin was olive and his hair black and silky. If it had not been for the blue eyes he could have passed as Spanish, helped in part by his fluency in the language after three years study at university. It was a talent he used with devastating charm when required. His rock band had been 'discovered' by a record producer and they had been offered an opportunity to lay down an album in Los Angeles. Josh had a healthy scepticism and a good education behind him so I had to trust his judgement that they would not be taken advantage of. So I kept my myriad objections to myself and gave them both my blessing.

Departure day loomed large and it was a typical Sydney winter's day, sunny and 23 degrees Celsius. Driving them to the airport they made a game of saying goodbye to things that they would miss as they had as children when we were leaving a holiday destination. Goodbye sparkling harbour, goodbye Opera House, goodbye Darling Harbour, goodbye Home nightclub, goodbye home. They had far too much experience at saying goodbye in their young lives. Goodbye baby Ben, goodbye Nanna, goodbye Grandpa, goodbye Dad.

"Goodbye Mum, I love you, will you be okay? I'll phone. I'll email everyday. I'm only fourteen hours away," Josh murmured in my ear as he embraced me in an enveloping hug. His arms felt so like his father's that my knees almost buckled.

"I'll SMS as soon as I land. I will email digital photos of the campus and my accommodation. I will send so many photos you will think you are living there too. You can come and visit me in the break and we can go and see Conan O'Brien together. You never know mum, now that we are no longer there to cramp your style some new man may sweep you off your feet."

Rebecca said all this without drawing breath and in her best reassuring style. She too hugged me and Josh joined in again. Here we were in front of the airport security gates in our own mini scrum. I ached with pride for the wonderful human beings they had become and with desolation for the coming loss.

"Remember how much I love you, be safe, have fun and don't worry about me. I have survived worse than this haven't I?" I reassured them.

They both ran back and hugged me again and I watched them disappear from sight, two faces struggling to find a balance between worry and excitement.

I tried to remember how my chic lit heroines handled the departure of the offspring from the nest. Alcohol, that was it, lots of it preferably with a good girlfriend or two. Well at least that was the technique used by the English and Irish heroines. The American heroines were either uptight or recovering alcoholics. Luckily I was an Australian and not a recovering alcoholic and I had a fridge stocked with my favourite Hunter Valley Semillon. A Thai takeaway, a girly DVD and a quick phone call to Sophie and Jess, my closest friends took care of the first night. But how to deal with the next 18,235 nights that I was most likely destined to live?

Night two was spent with a well-worn Chris Isaac CD and another bottle of Semillon.

Night three saw me consuming childhood comfort food—toasted cheese sandwiches and ice-cream and for variety a bottle of Chardonnay.

Night four found me sleeping in Rebecca's bed clutching her childhood teddy, the one she had already emailed and asked me to send to her.

Night five I moved to Josh's room where I smoked an old joint I found in his dresser drawer and listened to the Moody Blues on vinyl.

Night six was spent weeping into my pillow wearing Steve's old flannelette shirt washed so often it was baby soft but still retained his scent.

Night seven saw me wondering if I was an alcoholic, not yet in recovery.

Night eight I reread my old diaries from the time before I met Steve and in between sips of Shiraz (I had run out of white wine) I realised that I had once lived and loved without him or the children.

On the morning of the ninth day I awoke sickened by my orgy of self- indulgence and with a blinding reminder of why I did not usually drink red wine—the headache from hell.

But I also awoke with the germ of a crazy idea.

I dragged myself out of bed and into exercise gear in the hope that if I looked the part I might actually motivate myself to get to the gym. I spent the day looking the part and musing on my crazy idea without actually doing any exercise.

On day ten I actually went to the gym and succeeded in bypassing the local bottle shop with only a longing glance. Bathed in sweat and some exercise induced feel good endorphins the idea seemed slightly less crazy.

2

WHILE STILL A STUDENT AT UNIVERSITY I had travelled extensively throughout South East Asia on the hippy trail. I was a backpacker before backpacking became a lucrative business opportunity, when the local inhabitants would invite you for a meal or to stay in their homes for the novelty value or the pleasure of your company. I had travelled on the cheap through countries that we now liked to invade or were hot spots for terrorist training. I had embraced them all and my experiences with enthusiasm and idealism and recounted them in my diaries. But it was not the tales of the cultural differences, scenery and centuries old monuments that infected me with my crazy idea. It was love, my first love.

When I was nineteen I spent ten weeks of my university break travelling through Indonesia and Malaysia with a recently acquired university friend I had met in the language labs whilst attempting to learn Bahasa Indonesian. It was my first overseas trip and I was open to all new experiences. We travelled third class, caught local buses crammed with four times more people than seats and a variety of goats and chickens. We stayed away from Western hotels or restaurants and bedded down in small hotels and hostels, sharing rooms and sometimes beds with fellow travellers to cut costs.

We ate where the locals ate and what the locals ate; paper thin roti pancakes with curry sauce for breakfast, rice and noodles at other times; bananas and exotic rambutan for snacks with lots of hot chai sweetened with condensed milk. The hot showers and western toilets we deemed essential at home were non- existent and it became second nature to squat and bathe with tin cups of refreshing cold water. The most powerful memory from this time however apart from the smell of the durian fruit was of the day that I met Christian.

My girlfriend Sally and I were on the East Coast of Malaysia near the village of Rantau Abang. This was the late seventies and development had not yet reached here and it was truly idyllic, golden sands, palm trees, sunny and warm. Accommodation was basic, just our sleeping sheets on wooden benches in corrugated iron huts with thatched roofs.

We washed ourselves, wearing sarongs for modesty at the village well. There were travellers from around the globe—an Argentinean professor and his German writer girlfriend, an American born Thai girl, a French couple, a few Aussies, a madcap Irishman, two Canadian boys, and us. We had all been there for four days and bonded quickly as strangers do in strange lands. We had swapped travel tips, discussed politics and almost solved the world's problems. Life was much simpler when wearing a sarong.

On the fifth night of our stay a ferocious tropical thunderstorm hit. The rain came down in blinding torrents and as we all huddled under shelter we looked out on a solid curtain of water. Then as abruptly as it had started the storm stopped. The sun emerged again; steam started to rise from the ground and through the veil of mist emerged two very bedraggled young Englishmen who had been hitchhiking down the coast.

One of them was Christian. He was tall, very tanned with collar length blonde hair. He was wearing tailor-made calico trousers created from flour bags and they encased his long legs snugly. His faded light blue shirt was unbuttoned and revealed a chest that was smooth and hairless and he was very, very wet. His drenched backpack dropped to the ground with a loud squelch and he pushed his wet hair back from his face and shook himself like a dog. He grinned and revealed perfect white teeth and one equally perfect dimple in his right cheek. He blinked to dislodge the excess water in his ridiculously long lashes and turned in my direction and said "Hi!"

His eyes were green with golden flecks and his tanned face and white teeth seemed to have been created just to showcase the stomach churning beauty of those eyes. Even now when I thought of that first sight of him my stomach did a somersault and I could not help but smile. We introduced ourselves; we chatted; I fell in love. I'd had boyfriends before but had never experienced anything like this intoxicating feeling. I seemed to exist in an alcoholic-like haze where the sun shone brighter, music sounded sweeter and people around me were nicer.

It was the time of the annual Giant Turtle Migration and the next night by moonlight the giant leatherback turtles emerged from the ocean, lumbered slowly and ungainly up the sandy beach and laid their eggs. Their work done, their destiny fulfilled they returned to the ocean. The night was perfectly still and the full moon reflected on the sea and glinted off the turtles' ancient backs as they slowly plodded backwards and forwards on the beach. It was a primeval scene and the immense size of the 350 kilo turtles dwarfed all the onlookers and only hushed whispers could be heard.

It was against this backdrop that we shared our first kiss and it was like ***the*** first kiss, the beginning of time, the climax of the movie. It was almost too perfect.

Christian and his travel companion Ian were both English but very different. Ian was a thirty year old Londoner with a Master's degree in History and an ever increasing substance abuse problem. He would smoke, drink or otherwise imbibe any substance that could guarantee a high. Christian on the other hand although he enjoyed a drink found travelling itself enough of a high. He was from Cornwall and only nineteen and had been managing a supermarket to save enough for Art College when he threw it all in and decided to travel instead. He still hoped to paint one day and he carried a battered water colour palette with him. He painted quick studies of the beach and village and sketches of the people he met in a small notebook that he carefully wrapped in plastic and never let out of his sight.

His good looks and charm insured that he had left a trail of girlfriends behind him but he too said he had never been in love before this. The four of us travelled together for the next four weeks across to the west coast of Malaysia, down to Penang and on to Indonesia and Bali. We often shared a bed but sharing rooms with others and the religious sensibilities of our host countries did not lend itself to sex. So our relationship remained unconsummated until Bali.

Bali in the seventies was still largely a collection of sleepy villages but Kuta beach had a few larger hotels, a lot more western tourists and a more understanding Hindu population. So when we found rooms at a losmen at Kuta beach we took a room to ourselves and the luxury of a real mattress and a curtained window was liberating.

Christian was my first lover. I was an old fashioned girl in many ways and had always wanted my first time to mean something. Not for me the back seat fumblings at drive-ins. I wanted harps and violins and hopefully good sex and waking up to a boy I still loved in the morning. Well there were no harps but I am sure I heard violins and his body was so beautiful, smooth, muscular and hard in all the right places. We fitted together as though we were one and it was fun and never awkward. I felt as though I wanted him inside me always and for days afterwards I could still feel him there.

Suddenly I felt as though I was living and loving with a capital L. Time spent out of bed at this time seemed like a waste. We still went to the beach but it was really just foreplay. We ate our meals holding hands, he recited poetry to me in bed, we shared our innermost thoughts and he asked me to travel the world with him. We must have been quite sickening to those around us. When we had to part because I had to return home for my final year at university he had decided that he would follow me to Australia and work for a while. I had moved into a flat near the university the previous year so I envisaged a life of domestic bliss and sex interspersed with lectures and more sex.

The only thing that came true was the lectures. Christian's younger brother was killed in a motorbike accident in Cornwall two days after he arrived in Darwin; he did not even reach Sydney before he had to return home to support his mum. We wrote loving letters for many months but by the time I had saved enough money to visit him in England a year had passed and he had met someone else. An old school friend had been there to help him through his grief. She had helped him in that unique way that results in pregnancy and marriage.

I tried hard to hate them both but could only manage to half-heartedly despise and envy her. I still relished every day we had spent together but time and distance eventually worked their magic and I moved on, but no man until Steve ever inflamed my body or touched my soul in the same way.

Widowhood had left me sad, lonely, unemployed but financially comfortable. If I wanted to wallow in misery, travel or work part-time I could. Travel seemed like a preferable option. Wallowing was proving both boring and fattening. Although Steve and I had been to Europe and the United Kingdom before, it had always been for brief trips and we did little more than hit the tourist hotspots. I had not spent any amount of real time overseas since I was twenty. I certainly had the time now and for the first time in my adult life I had no ties of love or obligation to prevent me. I could not afford to board the QE11 for an extended cruise or spend three months at the Ritz but I could easily spend six months living and travelling in England.

Now this hardly seems like a crazy idea does it? Well my idea was merely contained in this desire—it was not the total sum of it. I was not yet ready to share this idea with anyone.

I arranged for Jess' young sister Zoe and her new husband to housesit for me. In return for paying for water and electricity they could live rent free for six months. My friends approved of my idea to travel; they believed a change of scene would be good for me. I believed they were also secretly relieved to have me out of sight for a while. My widowhood was a constant reminder of the vagaries of their own futures. If I was away they could be free from that niggardly guilt that they were not doing enough, that they had not included me in enough social events. They missed Steve too but I was unable yet to allow them a share of my grief.

The lure of overseas travel was also in part a desire to be free from others' expectations. Was I dealing with my grief according to the time line of the bereavement brochures? What was it, denial, anger, bargaining, acceptance in neat little time capsules? It doesn't work like that. One day there seems to be a future and the next the anger is again overwhelming. I wanted to be out of my normal environment so that I could do what I wanted without anybody's sad shake of the head and a comment about how out of character my behaviour was. I wanted to enjoy myself again without people commenting on how well I was 'getting over it'. I would never be over it because it was part of me.

My love, my loss, they were in my pores, in the blood that was pumping through my body, the blood that was pumping through my broken heart. But it was not all of me. I was not just the grieving widow, the mother of two amazing kids I was also the person that existed before all that. The person that had travelled and flirted and taken each day as it came, the person that had romantic ideals and no emotional baggage. It was that person I wanted to find again. It was the person who had fallen so easily in love with Christian. I knew she was there somewhere wanting to escape. And I believed that finding Christian might just help her escape. Now that *is* a crazy idea!

The logical part of my brain told me I was crazy, that I would never find him and if I did it would be disastrous. I knew that he was probably still married and more than likely would not even recognise me. Strangely I was not looking for romance or sex or love just an encounter with someone who knew who I was, not who I had become. And I convinced myself that it was not even the finding but the journey that was important. I told Josh and Rebecca that I planned to spend some time in England and they were pleased for me. We promised to keep in touch by twice weekly emails and phone calls.

Communication was so much easier in this digital age, nowhere ever seemed very far from anywhere else. In the 1970's and early eighties we had depended on postcards, aerogrammes and an erratic postal system. It was possible to be incommunicado from home for months. Phone-calls, always reverse charges, required some knowledge of foreign languages just to get through to an operator and were used in dire emergencies only. It was, in fact, wonderfully liberating. These days mobile phones are society's coitus interruptus. Sorry, can I call you back? I'm mid orgasm at the moment.

Of course technology has its advantages and I was very appreciative of them. I t was a relief to be able to have such regular contact with my offspring. I knew it would be a godsend to be able to send group emails to my concerned friends to assure them that I had not become a victim of the geriatric white slave trade. And of course it enabled me to do a sneaky cyber search on Christian. I googled him without success so at least I knew that he had not achieved worldwide fame. I checked International White Pages for his name and struck gold. Two hundred and seventy-five times in fact! I narrowed my search to a southern England radius and narrowed it down to seventeen possible entries. The internet, a stalker's best friend!

Of course, I told myself he may not even live in England anymore, or he may be bald, fat or even worse have grown back hair. I had no clear plan of what I was going to do and only a nebulous understanding of why. I knew I was quite mad and was cheered by the fact. I was very, very weary of being sensible and responsible. As mad as I was, I was not so mad as to tell anyone of my true intentions.

I decided to travel light so I only packed clothes that really suited me! I tried every outfit on in front of a full-length mirror and made sure each garment went with at least two other separates. I settled for great light weight pants in black and camel, one pair of dark bootleg jeans, a black jersey skirt dressy enough for evening, a knee-length denim skirt, assorted singlets and silk camisoles, a couple of soft cotton shirts, a cotton jumper and black jacket, a pair of casual shoes, black flats and killer black heels. Everything fitted into my carryon luggage and I was extremely proud of myself.

Unfortunately I had a stopover in Bangkok and a serious shoe fetish. So I reboarded the plane with an extra suitcase almost totally full of shoes and just those few totally essential items of clothing to go with them. After all there was no point buying strappy gold sandals and animal print mules without a couple of divine little tops to complement them.

3

I arrived in London at 6 a.m. on a glorious August Summer's day. It was in fact the start of an unusually warm and fine summer, the sort of summer that drove Londoners and tourists alike out of doors on any pretext. Blue striped deckchairs littered Green Park; couples in various stages of undress entwined themselves on the lawns and fed one another plump ruby red strawberries. People smiled as they queued for buses and were reluctant to enter the bowels of the London Underground when it meant sacrificing precious ultraviolet rays. People sat at sidewalk tables and expressed regrets that they had already booked their trips to Spain. It was even rumoured that the Queen was glimpsed in sleeveless attire.

I had booked into a small boutique hotel in Kensington and was very glad that I did not have a cat to swing as the poor thing would have been knocked unconscious while my elbow was still bent. It was however adequate for my needs as long as I did not wish to open the bathroom door and the wardrobe at the same time. I was almost regretting all those wonderful shoes but I was not regretting my decision to come. I was in no hurry to put my plan into action so spent many hours indulging my love of art. London has so many amazing galleries that I was transported even further out of my indulgent introspection. I was seduced by the Impressionists at the National Gallery and totally floored by the Tate Modern. I walked everywhere that I could and navigated the tube and the buses with ease.

The long twilight evenings rendered my discomfort at dining solo less intimidating as it seemed more like eating lunch than dinner. It is strange how a solitary lunch is quite acceptable but to request a table for one in the evening is seriously daunting. Thank god for half bottles of wine. I was proud of myself for my independence and when I rang the twins and told them that I was happy and enjoying myself it was almost true. I did miss conversation though and I started to become one of those annoying commuters who chat to trapped fellow passengers. The weather was so kind that no one seemed to mind and they seemed to expect it of Australians and far be it from me to contradict national stereotypes.

When I decided to leave London it was as much a need to see the ocean as it was a desire to try and locate Christian. The time away from home and my effortless days were starting to put a new perspective on my plans. I had always known that I was quite crazy but the limited chance of success in fact spurred me on. Logic told me that I would not be able to find him therefore emotionally I was safe. I could not be disappointed or rejected as I knew the task was impossible. But there was also that little smiling cherub that sat on my right shoulder and said "give it a try"; that same little cherub that reminded me of that little fluttery feeling I got when I remembered my first sight of him.

My next big decision was how to travel down to Cornwall, train, plane or hire-car. I liked the independence that car travel would afford but I also had a long-standing love affair with trains stemming from my childhood. I had enjoyed many journeys on steam trains when very young ensconced in a snug cabin. I loved to warm my toes on the foot-warmer while examining the black and white photos of country New South Wales that adorned the timber walls. I was thrilled by the heavy slam of the doors and the conductors cry of "all aboard" and sat either reading my comics or staring out the window and daydreaming whilst waiting with delicious anticipation for the stewardess with the food and beverage cart. In my memory it was very like the Hogwarts Express and just as magical.

However on this occasion my desire for greater independence and convenience won out and I feared that British Rail, as much as I respected it, would not live up to Harry Potter standard. So I hired a small sedan and set off for St. Ives. I had been very tempted by a Capri convertible but felt that to do a 'Thelma and Louise' without Louise was a little sad and as beautiful as the weather was at the moment it was still England and struggling with a soft-top on a wet motorway might be a little more than I could handle.

I had booked online into a small family run hotel near Porthmeor beach which thankfully lived up to expectation. It had eighteen rooms of generous size, by English standards, and boasted a magnificent view of the beach and was only a ten minute walk from the town. The beach actually exceeded my expectations with its white sands and surf. I almost felt that I was at home but the smaller scale of the beach and the surrounding cobbled streets placed it firmly in England.

I had chosen to start my search at St. Ives because it boasted wonderful art galleries and myriad smaller boutique galleries tucked around every corner. Artists had been coming here for decades because of the wonderful light, sort of like artistic moths. I was excited by the opportunity to visit Barbara Hepworth's sculpture garden and the new Tate Modern and if I chanced on a lead to Christian's whereabouts it would be an added bonus.

Knowing the likelihood of success had not stopped me from imagining our reunion. I 'd had plenty of time on the motorway to indulge my fantasies and in fact had to bring my rampaging mind back to the present when I found myself edging dangerously into adjacent lanes. I knew what I would be wearing. A floaty summer skirt just above the knees showed off my tanned legs and my wedge sandals gave me a little height and great calf definition. My recent pedicure would ensure that ten perfect polished toes would peek through my sandals. I was undecided about my top but all the imaginary garments showed a hint of cleavage and toned arms. My hair of course would be newly highlighted with warm copper tones and it would be thick and shiny and swing seductively as it brushed my shoulders. There were no humidity frizzes and bad hair days in my fantasy.

I would walk into a restaurant for lunch and confidently ask for a table for one and as I am shown to my table Christian who unbeknownst to me would be in the restaurant and also dining solo would look up intoxicated by the subtle perfume that followed in my wake. He would admire this attractive confident woman in the latest Dior sunglasses and his eyes would follow her to her table. As she sat and removed her glasses and surveyed the restaurant he would catch her eye and with a jolt of stunned recognition would be compelled to approach this goddess of loveliness. What happened after that I was unable to imagine.

Reality has however a way of getting in the way of fantasy or perhaps it is the other way around. I did in fact meet Christian although I don't think you could say that I found him, more that I bumped into him.

I spent many fruitless but enjoyable days at a variety of art galleries half expecting to see him around every corner or hopefully see an intriguing sketch or painting hanging on a wall with his familiar scrawl in the right-hand corner. I hoped that he would be an artist either struggling or established partly because it seemed so romantic but also because I knew that he had talent and would not feel fulfilled if he had failed to express it.

I spent one perfect and tranquil morning at Barbara Hepworth's gallery and gardens. Her garden gallery was enchanting with a variety of her sculptures scattered through it. You could walk around without any time restraints and sit and contemplate her wonderful works. You could touch her sculptures without officious museum guards pouncing and the feel of her work was amazing. The smooth cool texture of her brasses, the rough stone warmed by the morning sun were all intoxicating but calming to the senses. To sit there undisturbed and enveloped by her work felt like a return to the warm nurturing environment of the womb.

To complete this day of sensory overload I had booked in for a massage and facial at the spa on the hotel grounds. I was in the habit of washing my hair daily and wearing discrete but flattering makeup just in case at the next corner I caught a glimpse of Christian but knowing I was having a facial I had not shampooed my hair or bothered with make-up that day. On leaving the gallery I treated myself to a cappuccino and a slice of lemon cake dusted liberally with icing sugar in a cramped but charming coffee shop.

Like many cafes in St. Ives and indeed in Sydney too the walls were covered with small paintings for sale. As I ate my cake with gusto I simultaneously saw a painting I loved and started a sneezing fit from inhaling the icing sugar. My eyes were streaming and turning red and as I reached for my handbag to grab a tissue I spilt the remainder of my coffee over my white T-shirt and into my lap. I reached for the Indigo blue serviette to soak up the spreading stain on my top but as I rubbed the blue dye transferred itself to my shirt.

The chairs and tables were very close together and in my haste to find a bathroom in which to clean up I pushed my chair back into the table behind, tripped over the chair leg and found myself sprawled on the café floor. In falling I had upset the adjacent table and sent the china crashing to the floor.

I sat there stunned and humiliated with china shards embedded in my bleeding knees. From that vantage point however I could almost read the signature on the painting I had admired and I was sure it said C. Gilham.

My heart stopped momentarily as the café owners and other patrons rushed to my side. I apologized profusely offered my credit card to pay for any damage and enquired about the artist who had painted the haunting ocean scene. The owner, an attractive brunette in her forties looked up as the bell at the door tinkled and said,

"How amazing, he has just walked in!"

Panic gripped me; if it truly was Christian he could not see me like this. I needed to be serene and in control when we met. I needed him to see me as a mature reincarnation of my younger self not as the bedraggled sniffling bloodied loser I must appear now. I tried to hide my face behind my hair and keep my head down but as I stood and put weight on my left ankle it gave way and I reached out to stop myself from falling again. The only thing within reach was a shirt clad male arm and as I looked up from the depths of embarrassment to say "thankyou" I looked into a familiar pair of mesmerizing green eyes.

I couldn't speak. I stammered, mumbled and hobbled from the café as fast as my twisted ankle would allow. Just as the door shut behind me I heard the owner of the shirt clad arm ask the proprietor, "Was that woman Australian?" and then mutter softly under his breath "Julia?"

I reached the sanctuary of my hotel room after an agonizing twenty minute walk and collapsed on the bed and sobbed. I am such a fool, I thought, why did I even set out on this ridiculous quest. The past should remain just there, in the past. I have ruined everything. I even blamed Steve again. If he hadn't deserted me I wouldn't be in this ridiculous position. I should have been happy just to have had twenty good years with a wonderful man who truly loved me. But a voice inside me kept arguing, "you are not dead yourself, you still have to go on living."

As the wracking sobs left my body I made my way to the bathroom to wash away the blood, dirt and humiliation. The face that stared back at me was dirty and tear-stained and the upper lip was rimmed with a chocolate moustache from the cappuccino. I looked like the before version of the miserable people on *Extreme Makeover*. There were no more tears left so laughter seemed the only response.

I felt an overwhelming urge to share my humiliation with my girlfriends so wrote a long humorous email which I could not send as they had no idea what I was doing here. Then I thought some more, restructured the details slightly and told them that I thought the man in the café may have been an old boyfriend. I pressed send and felt in some way as though I had now committed myself to something. I was connecting however tenuously my two lives.

4

CHRISTIAN STOOD IN THE CAFÉ for some time thinking about the woman who had so abruptly left. She looked remarkably like an older and grubbier version of a girl he had known twenty-five years ago but the idea seemed too ludicrous to be true. He remembered the day they met and how sexy he had thought her sitting there with her long tanned legs curled under her. She had been wearing a transparent short pink caftan over a bikini and her hair had been long and half way down her back and the humidity had made it curl around her face. God, he thought I haven't thought about that day in years, but there sure had been some chemistry between them.

It was strange, he thought, how frequently she had popped into his head over the years. He had wondered how long it had taken her to find love again and he assumed she had married. He had in years past wondered what it would have been like to have still been together, especially when his own troubled marriage was at its lowest ebb.

His wife Rhonda had always accused him of being emotionally distant and immature and in his most honest moments he admitted to himself that if she had not been pregnant he would never have chosen to marry her. Twenty years ago he had such big plans. He was going to see the world and paint. He visualized himself as a twentieth century Gauguin, committing to canvas the ocean in all its different incarnations in a variety of exotic tropical locations.

When his brother Simon died he was torn between the desire to see Julia again and the need to be by his mother's side. His mother had brought him up single-handedly after his father's death and he loved her dearly. She was shattered by his brother's death; Simon had been her baby and she felt she had failed to protect him and she could not survive losing another loved one.

When six months had passed and he broached the subject of re-commencing his travels she just fell apart. By the time she was stronger and would have given him her blessing Rhonda was already pregnant and insisting on marriage. He had remained faithful to Julia for three months even though they had made no commitment to the future. He lived with the dream for months that somehow they would be reunited but life intervened and he was only twenty and sexual fidelity to a girl on the other side of the world, even a girl that he loved was too difficult.

Rhonda was an attractive blonde with a great figure and very popular with the local boys and when she showed more than a passing interest in him he was flattered. They had only dated for eight weeks when she announced she was pregnant.

The birth of Michael however changed everything. He did not know that it was possible to love a baby so much. It did not seem such a big sacrifice to postpone his dreams and provide for his child. His mother loved the baby to distraction and it helped fill the large void in her life. The early years of their marriage were good and Rhonda proved herself a very good mother, she was not however an easy person to live with. She needed constant validation of her attractiveness and desirability and he found it exhausting.

She was always checking his pockets and drawers for signs of infidelity and one day while visiting his mother she went through his childhood bedroom and found Julia's old letters. She went berserk. No matter how often he explained that their correspondence predated his marriage and the woman concerned was on the other side of the world she would not be placated. She burnt the letters but placed the ashes in a jar as a reminder, she said, of the love she should have had but was stolen by another woman.

He tried hard to give her what she wanted and lavished her with gifts and holidays they could ill afford. He made sure that he did more than his fair share of parenting so she could have time to herself but which she inevitably spent spying on him. She took to checking up on him and ringing his friends and work colleagues to confirm his whereabouts. The irony was that he had never strayed and was committed to his family and he had tried to love her even though she made it so difficult.

She did not want more children as she said they would only take more of his love away from her. To her the concept of love being expansive was alien. When Michael started school the situation improved and she got involved with many school committees. She was frequently out at night and started to dress with more care again. She had always been attractive but constantly told him that there was no point dressing up for him as he didn't love her anyway. There was less tension in the household now and she seemed happy. Christian was pleased that their relationship seemed to be improving and was genuinely happy that she seemed to be content at last. The peace was an illusion though and was abruptly destroyed by a phone call from a sobbing woman late one winter night.

Rhonda had been having an affair with the president of the school council and his wife, through sobs, was giving him all the sordid details. Christian's first response was disappointment that his peace had been shattered and anger that she had committed the infidelity of which she had unjustly accused him. He surprised himself that he did not feel hurt and he realised that the last remnants of love that he felt for her were gone.

When she returned home she first denied the accusation, then blamed him for driving her into the arms of another man and then sobbed and begged forgiveness and promised that it was over. He felt pity for her and did not wish to disrupt Michael's home life. Having been brought up by a single parent he felt strongly that if possible a child should have two parents.

Life resumed its monotony and they remained civil to one another. They still shared a bed and occasionally a sex life but there was no passion and very little tenderness. After fifteen years of marriage he wondered if this was all life was going to hold for him. He thought Michael was now old enough to cope with a marital split and wondered if he was brave enough to broach the subject with Rhonda. He was saved the angst of the decision however when he arrived home from work one Friday night to find her gone. Her car, her belongings and all the contents of their joint bank account were also gone. She left a note saying that she had finally found someone to really love her and he actually hoped that she had.

As the next five years rolled by he found life as a single parent was quite rewarding. Rhonda's 'someone to love her' turned into a succession of lovers over the years none of whom made her happy. At the disastrous end of each relationship she would cry on his shoulder and blame him yet again for the way her life had evolved.

He longed sometimes to return to a time when life was simpler and love and sex seemed spontaneous and pure. As he stood in the café remembering a young girl in a tropical land he felt refreshed. Could it really have been her?

5

THE FACIAL WENT A LONG WAY to restoring my wrecked face and the massage helped my injured ankle and the wine I had with dinner mellowed my feeling of embarrassment. I now knew that Christian really was in St. Ives and my instincts had been right and he did still paint. The glimpse I'd had was so brief but his eyes were too familiar for it too have been anyone else. I tried to recollect other details of his face. I remembered that his hair still fell onto his face and there were now lines around his eyes. The arm I had grabbed had been satisfyingly muscled and his body had lost the boyishness I remembered. Oh God, stop it, I thought as a tingle of warmth invaded my body. He is undoubtedly happily married with a tribe of gorgeous children. I hope his wife appreciates him. Surely though it wouldn't hurt to try and make contact and talk about old times if he hasn't forgotten all about me.

Did he really whisper "Julia" as I left or was it just the overworked imaginings of my fevered brain? How could he have seen the young me in the bloody dishevelled mess that I must have presented? Would it really help me to find out? The young carefree girl of the past was a lifetime away and my inelegant hurried departure may have burnt any bridge to the future.

When the dinner bill arrived I searched my wallet for my visa card and realised with a sense of dread that in my haste to leave the café I had left it behind. I paid the bill in cash but was flooded with another wave of humiliation when I faced the fact that I must return to the café to retrieve it.

Sleep proved elusive that night and when I did sleep my dreams were troubled by interchangeable images of Steve and Christian both offering an arm to lift me from the floor but each time I tried to grab onto an arm it would slip from my grasp and I would sink back into a heap. I didn't need Freud to find meaning in that dream.

I awoke the next morning with renewed determination. The humiliation I had suffered wouldn't kill me and I didn't know anybody here to point a finger and snigger and what if they did? I was a mature attractive woman of forty-something, the captain of my own ship, the architect of my own future. I was competent, capable and had already proved that I could handle 'the slings and arrows of outrageous fortune'. I was also extremely nervous and high as a kite on three double espressos. My mouth was having difficulty in keeping up with my brain. My hair was freshly shampooed, my makeup flattering, my grazed knees covered by form-fitting old Levis and my peacock blue silk cami showed just a hint of cleavage. It was time to face the café and my date with destiny and a visa card.

The weather had been glorious for weeks and I had got out of the habit of even considering the possibility of rain. Big mistake. I decided to walk the longer more scenic route to the café to help some of the coffee induced adrenalin recede to a more socially acceptable level and I passed an interesting looking gift shop I had not noticed before. Both Jess and her sister had birthdays within the next couple of weeks and if I bought gifts now I could get them posted back to Sydney in time. The shop had a wonderful array of unusual scented candles inlaid with ferns and wildflowers and miniature framed water-colours of the local scenery. I could visualize Jess relaxing with a glass of champagne in a bubble bath while inhaling the soothing perfume of the candles and for a moment I was flooded with a wave of homesickness, a longing not for the life I had left but for the life I had once enjoyed. My mood swings today were positively adolescent or I thought with horror, menopausal? The salesgirl though was delightful and gift-wrapped all my purchases with dried flowers and matching satin ribbons.

My shopping finished I set out once more for the café and noticed clouds rolling in from the ocean. I had always been fascinated by the changing face of the sea and the subtle colour palette created by the darkening sky was quite beautiful. I could smell and taste the salt spray on the strengthening breeze and I stopped in the cobbled street to saviour the sensation. After a few deep breaths I set off again, both arms laden with shopping bags and as I stepped around the next corner I was almost flattened by what felt like a mini tornado. The gentle invigorating breeze of a few moments ago had become gale force winds and driving rain and within seconds I was drenched.

My clothes were plastered to my body and my recently styled hair hung in damp ribbons to my shoulders and I just knew that my mascara was streaked down my cheeks. I felt like Scott of the Antarctic fighting his way through a blizzard and when I saw the welcoming lights of the café ahead I heaved a huge sigh of relief.

With both hands full I was forced to reverse into the closed café door bum first. Elegance was certainly not my middle name. As I turned around I saw a hand grab the door for me and I lurched into the room with my sodden shopping. I looked up through my bedraggled fringe to offer a watery smile of gratitude and found myself confronting once again those mesmerizing green eyes. Was this meeting to be a gift from the universe or a punishment for daring to hope?

6

CHRISTIAN HAD ALSO SPENT A RESTLESS NIGHT. As he tossed and turned in bed he cast his mind back with surprising ease to the bed he had shared with Julia in Bali. He had been shocked to find that she was a virgin, every girl he had been with before had been or pretended to be experienced. It felt like an awesome experience to be her first lover and the weeks they had spent getting to know one another before they first made love cemented the feelings he had for her. Although a virgin she was enthusiastic and sensual and every encounter they had was passionate but fun. There had never been any awkwardness as they explored each other's body. She had been so beautiful with her long slender legs and her high full breasts. He loved to watch her walk around their room topless with her long hair falling caressingly onto her breasts. They had been able to talk about anything. He admired her intelligence and her passion for life and she had been caring, kind and very funny.

He had been genuinely excited at the prospect of living with her in

Sydney. He wanted to see her in her own habitat and get to know her even better. He had longed to visit Sydney and surf at Bondi. He had an image of the city that was probably inaccurate but during the telecasts of the 2000 Sydney Olympics he had fallen in love with the place all over again. He had watched the Opening Ceremony with Michael and they had both loved the drama and humour it encapsulated. He had wondered at the time if Julia still lived in Sydney and was also watching. He'd had a foolish notion of a silver thread connecting them at that time. When he struggled into consciousness that morning he'd had such a strong visceral sensation that she was still lying beside him that he put his hand out to check. He was not convinced that the woman from the café had been Julia but he was determined to return there and see if they knew anything about her.

Christian sat in the café and drank a pot of Irish Breakfast tea. Merilyn, the owner was not in this morning and the other staff knew nothing of his mystery woman. It was not busy this morning so he could sit and watch the door on the off chance that she might come by without feeling as though he was depriving other patrons of a table. His first pot of tea had turned into a second and a crowd was building up when he felt obliged to vacate his table. When he stood to leave he peered through the misted window and saw an unfortunate woman struggling in the rain laden with shopping. He could not help but notice how transparent her wet clothes had become. He noticed with appreciation that her nipples erect with the cold adorned a set of full breasts and her damp jeans encased very shapely thighs.

His reverie was disturbed when her pert wet behind awkwardly pushed open the café door. He opened the door and prepared to leave when he looked down into the face that had haunted his dreams last night. He did not know how it was possible but an older and still beautiful Julia stood before him. He took the shopping bags from her, grinned and said,

"I'm not sure about the zebra stripes but getting rid of the moustache is definitely an improvement. Will I order coffee? Would you prefer it on the table or the floor today?"

And with that he took her arm, ushered her into the café and sat her at the table he had so recently vacated. He now had time to assess the face that accompanied the body he had so recently and blatantly been admiring. She wiped the water from her face and removed the worst of the mascara streaks. Time has been good to you Julia, he thought. Her skin was lightly tanned and there were a few more freckles dusting her cheeks and nose. Her slightly parted lips were still full and very inviting. Her body was curvier but only in the right places. Her eyes were clear and layered with varying hues of blue but overcast by shadows. She carries her years in her eyes, he thought, they have lost that gleam of mischief and adventure. But then she smiled and the years rolled back and the mischief returned to her eyes.

He looked down at her left hand and noticed she wore a wedding ring. Her eyes followed his gaze and she frowned briefly and when he looked up again he saw a hint of a tear in the corner of each eye. He took her hand in his and said,

"Well Julia, where have you been all my life?"

7

It's really him and here am I bedraggled again and shivering. Would it have been so difficult to meet him when I looked my best? My God, he looks gorgeous. His body has thickened slightly but those abs look great under his T-shirt. Those eyes, I could still drown in them, though I am probably already drowned. I didn't think you could get this wet without swimming. Even my subconscious is babbling now. Does he recognize me or is he just rescuing a damsel in distress? Come on Christian speak and then he grinned and that one perfect dimple in his right cheek ensnared me. He does know it's me.

"Moustache?" Oh! He did recognize me yesterday; well I'm passed embarrassment now. "Coffee would be great thanks and I only have it on the floor on odd numbered days." I replied.

He took my hand and I felt a slow fizz, like a Berocca dissolving in water, work its way up my arm. He touched my wedding ring and I had to fight hard to hold back the tears.

"Christian," I have finally said his name out loud after more than twenty years.

"You look great. Is it due to clean living or satisfying debauchery?"

I had dreamed of this moment for months but never really expected it to happen. I had tried to visualize how I would feel and how he would react. In my dreams the meeting was always conducted in an elegant restaurant and I looked my best, or even better than my best; I certainly was not wet and feeling embarrassed. Christian also had a scripted part to play. I knew his every response before he spoke, but here he was a real breathing and very masculine man.

The boy was still there but as I looked into those eyes and down to the freshly shaved jaw I realized I did not know this man at all. I felt awkward and not at all like the carefree confident girl he had known. Was he still married? Did he have children? How do I explain how I ended up at the bottom end of England all on my own? How honest can I be without appearing like a crazy stalker? The opening volley of conversation seemed easy but then the hesitation settled in. We both tried to speak at the same time then there would be an awkward lull as we each decided how to proceed.

I was starting to shiver from my damp clothes and so far all we had talked about were my impressions of Cornwall. I still felt the same physical attraction to him and could not take my eyes off his sensual mouth. He had beautiful full lips and I could imagine drowning in his kiss. Each time he smiled and showed his dimple little waves of pleasurable warmth invaded my body. I needed to get beyond this impasse of polite conversation.

"Christian," I loved the way his name rolled off my tongue, "let's play twenty questions before I develop pneumonia." He nodded a nervous assent.

"Do you have children?" I asked.

"One son, Michael, he's working in France at the moment." His face relaxed into pleasurable reflection as he answered.

"And your wife?"

"Long gone! I divorced seven years ago." He answered abruptly.

"I'm sorry," I said and part of me meant it while the other part secretly rejoiced.

"Steady girlfriend, significant other?" I bravely queried.

"No and No," he answered. My heart did little somersaults.

"Did you ever think about me?" I asked after a long pause. Please tell me yes or I will feel such a fool.

"Yes, I did." And then he looked directly into my eyes and said, "I even dreamt about you last night."

"I hope it was a good dream," I replied brightly but with a lump in my throat.

"It was a very good dream," and he lowered his lashes in remembrance and a broad grin erupted across his face.

I felt a blush that started at my hairline and made its way to my toes. He just grinned some more. How can this boy in a man's body have this effect on me, I wondered?

"My turn," he said as he pointed to my left hand. "You are married obviously."

"Widowed," I answered. "Four years ago."

"I'm sorry … was it a good marriage?" He asked tentatively.

"The best. He was a very good man, always there for me and the children. He had a gift for making you realize how much you mattered … he seemed to know the right word or the right touch to soften even the hardest times. " I answered fighting back tears again.

There was a pause before he replied and a look of self doubt crossed his face.

"You were fortunate to have found that. Not everyone is lucky enough to be loved in that way."

"Now tell me," he said raising the cup of now cold tea to his lips. "What brings you to my part of the world?"

I can't say 'you' that's too confronting and laden with expectation. He'll take out an apprehended violence order against me. I can see the headline now, *Antipodean stalker at large in Cornwall.Beware!*

"My twins are spending this year studying and working in The States so I decided to give myself a six month sabbatical. I started in London and have worked my way down. So I am footloose and fancy-free for a while." I answered.

"So running into me was just a happy accident?" He asked as his eyebrows raised in query.

"Yes it was just a random but fortuitous event." I replied with my fingers crossed. After all the actual 'running into' was accidental I reasoned. I then sneezed three times in quick succession and Christian said,

"I'm an idiot for letting you sit here like this you need to get into a hot bath before you get sick and ruin the rest of your holiday. Where are you staying?"

"At the Porthmeor Hotel. It has a wonderful view over the beach. I assume you know it?"

The rain had stopped and the sun was trying to gain the ascendance once more and I could delay my departure no longer so I stood to leave. As we reached the door we both went to speak at the same time.

"No, you go first". I stammered.

"No, no what was it you were about to say?" He countered.

I took a deep breath and said sheepishly,

"I think fate may need a helping hand to orchestrate another meeting. Would you like to have dinner with me tonight?" My heart hammered in my chest so loudly as I awaited his reply that I was convinced he must be able to hear it.

"The dining room at my hotel is very good." I suggested.

Time seemed to stand still and what was probably a moment's hesitation seemed like ten minutes.

"I would love too, but I can't tonight. How about tomorrow night, seven-thirty?"

I quickly answered yes and he took off and at such a speed that by the time I had picked up my shopping bags he was no longer in view.

I wonder what he is doing tonight and who he is doing it with? I was just leaving the café when the owner walked in and I remembered my credit card. I back tracked, retrieved it and apologised once again and she introduced herself.

"Don't worry about it. It was only a few cups. I'm Merilyn by the way. My staff tell me Chris, the artist who painted the picture you admired was asking about you. Did he succeed in tracking you down?"

"More or less. He just left in fact." I answered looking in the direction he had gone.

"He's a good looking man isn't he? The woman here are all half in love with him." She said smiling.

I tried to be excited about seeing him again but in a perverse and irrational way I was disappointed by his response. I had imagined our meeting and had assumed that he would just drop everything to now be by my side. I had not allowed for his hesitation. I had actually not allowed for his life at all. I knew so little about him. I had not asked about his job or even if he had one. Where did he live? I knew he still painted but did not know if he exhibited at galleries or only café walls. Oh, and I forgot to tell him how much I loved the seascape in the café. Had I talked too much about Steve for a first meeting? I sneezed again and Christian's advice about a hot bath seemed worth taking. The only thing I felt sure about was that I still fancied him like mad and when I remembered the look on his face when he recounted his dream I blushed again. I felt sure that there was still chemistry between us.

8

CHRISTIAN LEFT THE CAFÉ AT A RUN. He had thirty minutes to get home pick up his car and collect Michael from Newquay airport. He was returning from Paris and bringing home a girl Christian had yet to meet. I can't believe that I forgot, he thought, and I didn't get any food in. I'll have to take them out to dinner. He grabbed his car keys and set off on the A30. He would be late but not very, he thought. Sitting behind the wheel and stuck behind a truck he allowed himself to think of Julia again. She was as beautiful as ever.

He thought of her breasts beneath the revealing wet singlet and found himself becoming aroused. Christ, he thought, I do not want to meet Michael's girlfriend while sporting an erection. Concentrate on her eyes he thought. He had been fascinated by her eyes when they first met. It was as though multiple tones of blue had been layered in them. Her eyes reflected her moods the way the ocean reflected the changing sky. He knew from experience that passion turned them the deepest ocean blue; while hap-

piness made them appear like the midday sky. The grey he saw in them today reminded him of a stormy sea and the uncertainty it threatened.

He was not convinced she was in Cornwall by chance but his ego would not allow him to believe that she had come in the hope of seeing him either. When she talked of her husband he felt pangs of jealousy and inadequacy. He had never made any woman feel that special or secure, as Rhonda had repeatedly pointed out. The only relationships in his life where he knew he could not be found wanting were with his mother and his son.

There had been many relationships though, sometimes just for sex and sometimes out of loneliness but he was never able to give the women what they wanted. There had always been something missing. He had felt trapped for so many years that he could not make that leap into commitment again. He handled carefree, no strings attached sexual relationships with gusto but felt unable to be the bedrock that most women he'd dated had seemed to need. He wasn't lying when he told Julia that he was footloose and fancy free, he had worked very hard to maintain that state.

He pulled into the airport carpark just as Michael and his girlfriend wheeled their bags through the double glass doors. Michael recognized the car and they made their way over to Christian. Michael at just twenty-four was very like his father at the same age. The same long lean legs and even the same loping gait. He was a few inches taller but his hair was blonde and straight and cut quite short at the moment. He had his mother's blue eyes but when he smiled he was his father twenty years ago with that same beguiling dimple animating his already attractive face. He was dressed in jeans and white T-shirt which showcased his broad shoulders and his well defined chest and he held the hand of an attractive brunette girl.

"Dad, I would like you to meet Madeline," said Michael proudly.

"And Madeline this is my father."

"Bonjour Monsieur Gilham it is a pleasure to finally meet you," said Madeline as she kissed Christian on both cheeks.

"A pleasure for me too Madeline and please call me Chris."

"Certainement Chris." She answered with a smile.

"Have you been to Cornwall before Madeline?" Christian asked as he helped stow their bags into the back of his aging Volvo station wagon.

"Non, it is my first time but Michael has talked about it so often I feel as though I know it very well." She answered.

As she climbed into the back seat of the car and bent to do up her seatbelt Christian gave Michael a thumbs- up of approval and the grin on Michael's face grew even wider.

As they pulled out of the carpark and made their way back to the A30 Christian sneaked furtive glances into the rearview mirror. She really is an extremely attractive girl, he thought. She had flawless skin with a light summer tan and a flush of colour accentuating her high cheekbones. Her hair dark and shiny was cut into a severe geometrical bob which highlighted her fine dark eyes dramatically. She was dressed in dark blue jeans tucked into high heeled brown boots and a navy and white boat neck Tshirt. The well worn soft brown leather bag which she had carried over her shoulder now sat snugly in her lap. Michael pointed out landmarks along the way and she responded with enough enthusiasm to please him. Christian could tell at his first glance at Michael that he was in love with this girl. I hope she feels the same way, he thought.

They pulled into the gravelled driveway of the cottage within forty minutes. The cottage had a wonderful aspect and Christian had remodelled over the years and the back of the house was now almost entirely floor to ceiling windows. The freeform cottage garden gave way to undulating grassy sand dunes and stunning views of the estuary.

Max, Michael and Christian's loved old pointer scrambled excitedly from his bed by the back door. His tail thumped loudly against the glass and as Christian let him in his nails clomped loudly across the burnished timber floorboards as he raced towards his younger master. After Michael had given him the required scratch behind his velvety ears Max tentatively sniffed Madeline's proffered hand. Satisfied that she was friend not foe he demanded a scratch from her also.

Christian was pleased to see that Madelaine was a dog lover and had gained Max's approval. He had always believed that dogs were quite good judges of character. Another thumbs up for Madeline, he thought.

The kettle was on and the young couple had retired to Michael's old bedroom to unpack. Max however had other ideas and grabbed his lead from the laundry and then trotted off to find Michael and Madeline. He found them sitting on the bed holding hands and kissing so he jumped up and pushed himself between them and presented them with the lead. They both laughed and took the not very subtle hint.

"I think we are being conned into a walk Madeline. We can walk down to the estuary and breathe in the salt air if you feel up to it." He suggested.

"I would love to, just let me change my shoes and use the bathroom first." She said as she bounced on to her feet. Michael wandered out to the kitchen, followed by Max still trailing his lead.

"We are going for a walk Dad. Max has a date with a seagull I think," Michael said as the dog loudly shook his lead to remind them of his presence. "Well, what do you think?"

"I'd no idea he was even seeing one!" replied Christian.

Michael raised his eyes to the ceiling and said "Dad!"

"She is a very beautiful young woman Michael and I am looking forward to getting to know her better. Max is already won over and I always trust his judgement."

9

I WAS DETERMINED to look gorgeous the next time we met and tried on every combination of every garment in my suitcase. I placed two possible outfits on the chair but would leave the final decision until tomorrow night. I was still restless after my room service meal and decided to get some fresh air and some ice-cream. It was a beautiful night and the air felt even fresher after the rain. I strolled along contentedly licking my strawberry gelato looking into the variously lit restaurant windows and trying hard not to envy all the cosy couples when I saw a silhouette I recognised.

Christian was sitting alone at a table idly twirling a wine glass. My stomach leapt into my throat as my eyes greedily gorged themselves on his image. His hair looked freshly washed and fell over his forehead as he leant forward. He was wearing a blue striped shirt, dark trousers and sports jacket. He had obviously taken trouble with his appearance and looked good enough to eat. I debated wether to pop in and say 'Hi' but thought he might think I had stalked him when this time the encounter was genuinely accidental. As I reluctantly dragged my gaze away and began my journey back a stunning young woman with a gorgeous geometric haircut, a Nefertiti neck and cheekbones you could cut ice with walked elegantly across the crowded restaurant and straight to his table.

When he saw her he leapt to his feet and took her hand while she leant in to kiss him. I was mesmerised. She was so utterly stunning and stylish. Her black jersey dress plunged dramatically at the back and revealed flawless skin. It skimmed her knees and showed to advantage her beautifully shaped calves and pedicured feet encased in black strappy Jimmy Choos. I recognised the shoes because I had bought the cheap Thai knock off version, *Jimmy Achoo* in Bangkok. No wonder he couldn't dine with me tonight he had a date with a goddess.

I felt such a fool to have even contemplated that a man as gorgeous as Christian would have been interested in a woman his own age. Good looking men seemed to just get better looking with age, wrinkles and grey hair just added character. I felt old and saggy and when I compared my freckly Aussie skin to the flawless complexion of the goddess I felt even more defeated. There was nothing in my suitcase that could hold a candle to her simple black dress. Even my strawberry gelato could console me no longer I needed the big guns, a family sized block of chocolate and an ego boosting talk of cheering platitudes from a good friend. I checked my watch and calculated that I should be able to catch Jess in her lunch break right after I self medicated with mini bar M&M's.

I surprised myself by sleeping well and awoke feeling positive and energised. The sun was shining, the ocean was sparkling and I was ravenous. I had been denying myself a full English breakfast for weeks but today I was going to indulge and swim it off later. I still felt there was something to explore with Christian and I convinced myself that the chemistry I had sensed was real. I was going to follow my instincts and silence the negative thoughts in my head.

I visualised again the almost photographic image I had captured of the 'goddess' and decided that if he wanted elegant sophistication I too could give him that, although it would take me twice the time to look half as good. I imagine that she just brushed her hair and threw on any old thing and still would turn heads wherever she went

As I made my way down to the breakfast room I saw a notice outside the dining room. *Closed tonight due to special function.* I must let Christian know, I thought, but how? I had no way of contacting him. What if he doesn't ring me? What if he doesn't turn up tonight? Positivity was leaching out my pores with every breath. Stop it! Enjoy your breakfast, enjoy the beach and let the rest unfold! I actually took my own advice and enjoyed my day immensely.

I swam laps at the beach and with my face protected from the sun soaked up some unusually hot English sunshine. I admired my tanned legs and let the sand run through my fingers. I had always found it hard to stay unhappy when I was wet and salty and could feel the heat of the sun soaking into back muscles fatigued from swimming. It provided a sensory overload that banished negative feelings and opened the mind to endless possibilities. The most taxing thing I had to do that day was to transform the casual sun loving creature that I truly was into the elegant sophisticated woman that I hoped was hiding just under the surface. After a day spent indulging the senses I felt up to the challenge.

I had a long hot shower and shampooed and conditioned my salt crusted hair. I exfoliated my face and body with a gorgeous rose scented scrub I had purchased at the gift shop yesterday. I shaved my legs and underarms and lavishly moisturised every inch of skin. Today's sun had slightly deepened my light tan and the swim had toned my arms and legs. I felt good and when I stood naked in front of the mirror I didn't recoil in horror from the image. I replaced the outfits I had considered earlier and brought out the big guns.

I'd bought a midnight blue silk dress in a London sale. It cost more than I would normally pay but I had fallen in love with the colour and the sales girl had said it enhanced my eyes. I was deciding on shoes and accessories when the phone rang. I flung myself across the bed in a hurry to answer it, hoping that it was Christian and dreading that he may be ringing to cancel. It was reception asking if I knew a Mr. Gilham. He had asked to be put through to an Australian called Julia but as he did not know my surname or room number they were a little suspicious. I accepted the call happily.

"Hi!" I said with enthusiasm if no originality.

"Hi! Are we still on for tonight? Or have you perhaps run in to another old boyfriend?"

"No, you are the only one this week. The hotel dining room is closed tonight though. Any other suggestions?" The image of breakfast in his bed loomed large and inappropriately in my head.

"Leave it with me, I'll pick you up at 7.30pm. And Julia?"

"Yes?" I answered with dread and anticipation.

"What's your surname now?"

"Kennedy." I said and suddenly Steve was in the room there with me and things seemed very crowded.

10

CHRISTIAN WAVED MICHAEL AND Madeline off as they went to dinner at Ben's place. Michael and Ben had been like brothers since their first day at school and had found it no hardship to maintain their relationship since. Ben too was an only child and they had each been like the sibling the other had lacked. Michael was uncharacteristically nervous and hoped that Ben would find Madeline as beautiful and wonderful as he did. It was important to him that these two people that he loved would also grow to love one another. On a purely superficial level also he wanted Ben's jaw to drop when he saw her for like all sibling relationships there had always been an element of competition.

Michael wondered what was going on in his father's life. He had seemed a little distracted today and when they had asked if he wanted to accompany them to Ben's he had thanked them for the invitation but said he had a prior engagement He offered no further details and Michael did not want to press him in front of Madeline. He hoped there was a woman in his life again for he deserved to be happy and it had been such a long time since any woman had contributed to his happiness.

Michael loved his mother but was the first to admit she was not the sort of woman to make a man happy for very long. His face darkened as he thought of introducing Madeline to her for she was hypercritical of other women and had been jealous of all his previous girlfriends. Still, time enough for that, he thought. I haven't even popped the question to Madeline yet. He loved her deeply but was not sure if she would say 'yes'. This long weekend had been a trial run to see if they could fit into one another's lives; to see if their love would survive outside of his Paris apartment. He looked across at her sitting contentedly beside him in the car. She turned and smiled and his heart swelled and suddenly he did not care what anybody thought of her. He loved her and that was all that mattered.

Christian dressed with more care than usual and wore the pistachio green French linen shirt that Michael had given him for Christmas. He wavered between jeans or dress pants but opted for the more casual look of jeans as Julia still seemed to be a very casual girl or woman, he corrected himself. He also secretly thought that he looked sexier in jeans. He had been told once by some long ago date that his butt looked good in jeans and he had retained the information if not the woman's name. He had no preconceptions about where the evening may lead but he felt young and excited and his life suddenly seemed to offer unlimited possibilities.

He parked in the carpark behind the hotel and thought they could leave the car there and walk to the restaurant as it would be impossible to park any closer on a busy summer night. He entered the hotel and approached the reception desk in order to buzz her room when Julia walked down the stairs. He almost didn't recognise her. She was breathtaking.

She was wearing a dark blue silk shirtmaker dress that shimmered in the light when she moved. The deep V neckline showed generous cleavage and the wide silver belt highlighted her narrow waist. Her legs were bare and tanned and she wore very fragile looking silver sandals that wrapped invitingly around her elegant ankles. Her hair was up in some sort of casual style with tendrils around her face. She wore very unusual sapphire and silver drop earrings and a sapphire pendant that framed her face and brought attention to her décolletage. Her eyes looked vibrant and reflected the blue of the dress and jewellery and she looked so beautiful she took his breath away.

Her elegance and sophistication intimidated him a little; this was not the girl he had known. It may have been chauvinistic of him but he quite liked her looking dishevelled and vulnerable yesterday as it made him feel protective and in control. He felt as if he was on a blind date and his date looked unlike the image his brain had created. He was going to enjoy getting to know this woman but he felt insecure and wondered why such an attractive woman was even interested in him, if indeed she was he added as an afterthought.

Christian looked nervous and totally sexy. His pale green shirt made his eyes even more striking. I wondered if he had chosen it for that reason. Perhaps some sales girl had flirted with him and told him how gorgeous he looked in green. Well done if she had for she was spot on. His jeans fitted snugly and hugged a great looking butt; he had certainly kept in shape. I had this sudden urge to slip my hand into his back pocket and give the perfectly formed buttock a little squeeze but resisted the temptation valiantly. When I passed the mirror in the foyer I glanced at my reflection furtively and was surprised to see a beautifully dressed attractive mature woman and not the insecure creature that lurked beneath. Still, I did not recoil from the reflected image and that was twice in one day, surely a new world record.

Christian took my hand kissed me on the cheek and told me I looked beautiful and asked if I liked Italian. We walked a few blocks over the cobble stoned streets; actually I teetered precariously in my ridiculous but beautiful silver heels to La Luna Trattoria. I realised with alarm that this was the same restaurant where I had seen him last night. He must get some sort of bulk deal for dates, I thought. Dine with one woman feed the next one for free sort of deal.

After we were seated I asked with studied nonchalance,

"Do you dine here often?"

"Yes, I do actually. The three of us ate here last night."

"Three?" I queried. Don't tell me the goddess has a twin sister.

"My son Michael and his girlfriend Madeline, they are here for the weekend. Actually they remind me of us a little at that age. You know, can't keep their hands off one another, long lingering glances, that sort of thing. Love seemed so uncomplicated then didn't it?"

Christian said looking not at me but an image from the past.

I felt cheered and foolish and suddenly a whole lot more relaxed. The waiter poured the first of many glasses of Chianti and we worked our way through a wonderful antipasto platter. We talked of his art and his plans to open a gallery in a vacant shop nearby. As he talked of his plans the years rolled back and his boyish enthusiasm bubbled to the surface. He had recently inherited some money from a childless uncle. A very handy thing to have in the family I thought; the generous childless relative should be compulsory. I wonder if the U.N could legislate for such a thing. I restrained from sharing this thought in case they had been very close. It was at this point in my imaginings that I thought I had better slow down my alcohol intake.

Our pasta mains were delicious and as we tasted each other's meal there were enough long and lingering looks to give Michael and Madeline a run for their money. By the time tiramisu and coffee arrived we were into Olympic flirting and when he entwined his fingers with mine across the table a wave of warmth invaded my recently groomed bikini-line. I longed to run my fingers through his sun streaked hair and across his shaven chin. The candle-light accentuated his chiselled features and my eyes which were becoming slightly hard to focus could not draw themselves away from his beautifully inviting lips. When he suggested a walk to the beach I happily concurred and hoped the fresh air would sober me up a little.

I t was a beautiful night. The air was still warm, twilight had passed and the moon shone over the ocean. Christian looked even better by moonlight. My elegant look however seemed to be dissipating in increments. My up hairdo had come down and my hair messily brushed my shoulders and my sandals were now off and I could feel the cold sand between my toes. The gentle breeze made me shiver and Christian put his arm around me.

"Do you remember our first kiss Julia? On the beach, in the moonlight, just like this," he said with obvious intent as he leaned closer.

As he drew me in finally for the kiss I had been waiting all evening for I became so aroused that I could feel my thighs vibrating and I said in tipsy awe and wonderment,

"Can you feel the vibrations too?"

"I can actually ... I think it's your mobile ringing."

Feeling like a fool yet again I reached into my purse to turn it off. I wanted nothing to mar this moment. I briefly glanced at the screen before turning it off and realised it was Rebecca. My daughter rarely rang me; we usually exchanged sms or emails so my mother's instinct took over and I knew something was wrong. I mouthed "sorry" to Christian "it's my daughter," and as soon as I flipped the cover the air was rent with sobs.

"Mum, mum, Pete and I broke up. The bastard had been sleeping with his ex every time he went home. I was just his college fling, just a taste of exotic Aussie. I feel like an idiot. Why wasn't I enough for him?" She asked pleadingly.

Rebecca had been seeing Pete for about three months and he was her first serious relationship. She had emailed me photos and he was certainly very good looking. He had told her that they had a "magical connection" and she was his muse. The sobs started to lessen and she apologised for upsetting me. With every fibre of my being I wanted to be beside her, holding her close, stroking her hair and reassuring her that she was lovable. I wanted to make her comforting hot chocolate as I had done when she was younger. She had already suffered too much loss in her life and my heart ached at the thought of her future disappointments.

"How about I fly over for a lightening visit?" I tentatively suggested. I wanted her to know how much I loved her and missed her but I didn't want to undermine her new found independence.

"No, I'll be okay mum. I think I just needed to cry and get it off my chest. I'll go and stick pins in his photo instead. His hairline was starting to recede anyway. He'll probably be bald by the time he's thirty." She said with a return of her fighting spirit.

"You know that he doesn't deserve someone as wonderful as you don't you?" I reassured in typical mum but genuinely meant fashion.

"Yeah I know. I really wish I could talk to dad. He always seemed to know what to say didn't he? Thanks for listening. I hope I didn't disturb your night. What were you doing anyway? This line is not very clear, you sound a bit drunk!" She said with a chuckle.

I looked at Christian patiently standing by with a look of concern on his handsome face and said,

"Nothing honey, I just finished dinner and went for a walk on the beach."

"You shouldn't be walking on your own at night, even at your age, it can be quite dangerous." She scolded.

Our roles had reversed in the blink of an eye and I felt amused but every one of my years. I assured her I was not alone but had run into an old friend.

"Oh, well I guess two women walking together are safer. Mum, I have to go I'm running late for a tutorial. We have our first exhibition coming up soon. I'll email you the details. It would be cool if you could come. You must be getting sick of all that solitude by now. Thanks for the shoulder to cry on. I love you, bye."

"I love you too. Ring me anytime. I don't mind wet shoulders." I reassured as I hung up.

I put my phone back in my purse and apologised to Christian. I felt disappointingly sober now. The moon had disappeared behind a cloud and the temperature had dropped. Christian wrapped his jacket around my shoulders and I snuggled into his comforting chest but the mood like the moon had gone and I felt sad and deflated.

"I'll walk you back to the hotel." He said and his reassuring arm stayed firmly around my shoulders as we walked back.

"Parenthood is not easy is it, especially on your own," he said with the voice of experience. At the entrance to the hotel he said goodnight and pecked me chastely on the cheek. I felt like his maiden aunt. We swapped mobile numbers and he said he would call. I watched him walk away in his familiar loping gait and I admired his taut behind once more. I felt those vibrations again but this time my phone was not ringing.

Christian was not sure how he felt. All night through dinner he had been stimulated by Julia's insightful comments about art and her wry humorous outlook on life. He could feel the erotically charged atmosphere between them and with each glass of wine she drank he was reassured to see the veneer of sophistication slipping. She was so earthy and sensual and when he took her hand he could see her eyes deepen in colour as she too became aroused. This simple contact was more erotic than any he had felt for years. The curve of her breasts under her shimmering dress inflamed his senses. It amazed him that at only five-foot-five she looked so becomingly long-legged. When she talked of swimming laps at the beach the image of her in a bikini had him shallow breathing.

The moon reflecting on the ocean felt so like that long ago night in Malaysia that it seemed as if fate had contrived to turn back time for them. He could feel her longing for him, her longing for the touch of his lips and he wondered once they kissed if he would be able to draw back afterwards. He was not to find out for the moment was shattered by the shrill cry of her mobile.

He was disappointed and frustrated at the disruption to their evening but also relieved at his reprieve. He was not sure if he wanted to become involved with someone with so much obvious emotional baggage and a complicated life. He had spent so long avoiding real commitment he was not sure if he was capable of it. He wanted to make love to her with every fibre of his being but he did not think he was ready for what it might mean. He cared about her he realised and did not want to hurt her again but he also felt so young and happy when he was with her and he wanted to capture and keep that feeling. He was aware that if he had have pressed the issue she would probably have invited him back to her room and he was sure the mood could have been rekindled very easily but she was in such an emotionally fragile state after her daughter's call that he knew her judgement would have been impaired.

He wanted to see her again but felt they should talk about what they both were looking for. Then again he thought, there had perhaps been too much talking in both their lives and what was required was a therapeutic and mind blowing fuck.

11

I AWOKE TO THE SOUND of my mobile ringing and groggily answered it half expecting it to be Rebecca again but the voice was decidedly male.

"Hope you slept well and no hangovers I hope. It is a glorious day outside and I would like to take you on a picnic, if you are up for it."

"Australian women don't get hangovers! But I will admit to a slight headache. I'm sorry about last night Christian. I did not mean to drink so much. I hope I didn't say anything too embarrassing."

I cringed inwardly as I remembered my line about "feeling the vibrations." It would have made a great punch-line for a blonde joke.

"A picnic would be wonderful though. It might clear the remaining cobwebs from my head. What time and what can I bring?" I asked hoping he would say in about two hours so I could luxuriate in bed a bit longer.

"A swimsuit and a sense of adventure should suffice. I'll pack the picnic hamper. Pick you up in an hour?"

He then hung up while I languidly stretched and imagined his long tanned legs stretching beside me. My libido seemed to have been given a kick start at the sound of his voice. I loved his voice and always had, it had a lyrical quality that age had improved. The timbre had deepened and had a Daniel Craig quality to it, he sounded just plain sexy. In fact I found everything about him a turn on and this gave me cause for concern. I had not even kissed a man since Steve died and I worried that if I didn't have sex soon I might implode but I also feared that if I did I was in danger of exploding in spectacular fashion—and explosions caused far reaching, unpredictable aftershocks.

I found my beach bag and threw in sunscreen, a hat and the slightly damp bikini I had worn yesterday. I rummaged through my rapidly dwindling pile of clean clothes but was relieved to find a pair of unworn white shorts and a red and white striped shirt. I slid into a pair of white Keds and spritzed my hair with beach-hair product as I did not have time to style it. I applied a touch of tinted moisturiser, mascara and lip gloss and slid on my Gucci sunglasses. The image in the mirror was reasonably reassuring apart from my knees which were still slightly grazed from their close encounter with the shattered coffee cups a few days ago. I'll do, I thought. I popped a couple of paracetamol with a cup of tea and hoped Christian had packed plenty of food as I was starving.

Christian was waiting for me again when I went downstairs. Punctuality appeared to be one of his virtues. I hoped it was a result of his eagerness to see me. He was wearing khaki cargo shorts, a white T-shirt and old but clean sandshoes. His aviator sunnies were pushed back on his head and with his hair off his face his stunning green eyes drew even more than their usual share of attention. He smiled and flashed that disarming dimple and I suddenly had an even greater spring to my step. The middle-aged receptionist gave him an appreciative glance and I felt quite proprietorial. He took my bag and escorted me to an old yellow Capri convertible with the top down. The picnic hamper sat snugly on the back seat.

"Wow!" I said, "This looks like fun, although it's not what I imagined you driving."

"Not mine I'm afraid. I borrowed it from a friend to impress you. Are you impressed?" Christian asked after a pause.

"Very. If the hamper is of a similar impressive standard I may have to recommend you as a tourist attraction to all single Aussie women visiting Cornwall."

"I'm actually finding one is enough of a handful. Not that I have had a handful yet." He said pointedly after a pause and his dimple flashed again and I melted a little more. At this rate I would be nothing but a pool of liquid on the seat of the convertible before we even reached our picnic spot. Christian would have to have the car detailed before he could return it to its owner.

It was indeed a beautiful day and I closed my eyes to enjoy the warm sun on my face and the salty breeze in my hair. Each time Christian reached down to change gears our fingers touched and little shots of static electricity coursed up my arm. I was mesmerised by his arms, by the way the short golden hairs moved in the breeze. I studied the branch like veins that traversed his arm and noted how prominent they became with each movement. I wanted to trace their intricate patterns with my fingers, I wanted to sketch them, to somehow capture this moment. I felt if I could capture it I could keep it to sustain me in darker times. Experience had taught me to enjoy these fleeting moments of contentment for the permanence of happiness had proven to be illusory.

We drove through one picturesque fishing village after another and finally parked the car atop a cliff where Christian said on a clear day you could see the Isles of Scilly.

We clambered down a steep cliff face to a secluded bay with water gently lapping the seaweed strewn shore. I felt that I had been here before but knew with certainty that it was impossible. Realisation dawned in a rush.

"You've painted this spot. This is the seascape on display in the café isn't it? You captured it so perfectly Christian." His eyes lit with pleasure at my compliment

"I've painted it many times. My brother and I used to explore down here when we were kids. There is a cave on the other side of the cliff we loved to play in. We fancied ourselves as pirates or those adventurous kids from Enid Blyton. I used to come down here on my own after he died, I feel closer to him here than anywhere else."

He looked out to sea remembering a different companion and sighed before turning to me and saying, "You have a good eye Julia to recognise this place." I put my hand to his face and stroked his cheek.

"Thankyou for bringing me here. You are fortunate that you have somewhere that you feel close to Simon." I said as I drew back.

"I know what a painful time it was for you when he died, trying to help your mother while dealing with your own loss. I could almost wring the tears out of the letters you wrote to me during those months ... I wanted to be by your side so badly then you know."

"I know you did. The distance seemed much greater then. The world is a smaller place now, thankfully." He said as he smiled at me.

I think we both contemplated for a brief moment how different our lives would have been if Simon hadn't died or I had come over to be with him. But I could not imagine a life where I had not loved Steve. Whatever grief loving him had created every second of it had been worthwhile.

As we unpacked the picnic hamper I told him I was indeed suitably impressed. There were smoked salmon sandwiches, goat's cheese and tomato quiches, fat black olives and a wedge of brie cheese, muscatel grapes and juicy ruby red raspberries. When he unpacked blue rimmed china plates and navy blue napkins and fine glass champagne flutes I remained impressed but at least I knew now that he had not created this feast himself. I recognised the china and the unfortunately coloured napkins.

"You have outdone yourself Christian this is magnificent. Give my regards to Merilyn when you return the china to the cafe won't you."

"It was the napkins that gave me away wasn't it? I should have requested white ones. Can I tempt you with a glass of Bollinger?"

He asked as he produced the bottle of perfectly chilled champagne. You can tempt me with more than that I hope, I thought as I presented my glass to be filled.

We were both equally hungry and demolished the picnic fare quickly. We had drunk half the bottle of champagne when he suggested a swim. I ducked behind a rock and changed into my bikini. I knew that I did not look twenty but my arms were toned and my tummy flat. My breasts were not as perky as in youth but they were still full and the stretchmarks on my hips, a legacy of carrying twins, were camouflaged by my tan. I had a sudden fear that Christian might be a speedo wearing guy. I did want to see more of him but not through lycra. My fears were allayed when I saw him appear in a pair of very suitable hibiscus print navy board shorts.

He was tanned and his chest was well muscled with a triangle of golden hair. He may not quite have had a six pack but his abs were well defined and he carried no excess body fat. He looked fit and very masculine and just peeking above his boardies on his left pelvic bone was a small tattoo. I recognised it as a Hindu mandala and I remembered how fascinated he had been with such imagery. Clothes may maketh the man but he looked even better without.

He unashamedly looked me up and down and I blushed and thumped him on the arm like a schoolgirl.

"Could you be a little less obvious?" I said and raced into the water. The waves were small and I dived in and out them with abandon. He followed behind me and we frolicked like kids. He caught me in the shallows and pulled me close and his mouth sought mine. He kissed me tentatively at first then with more ardour. His tongue explored my teeth and mouth and I could feel him stiffen in his board shorts. I responded hungrily and melted into his kiss. A larger wave rolled in and tumbled us onto the sand. In my mind I was picturing Deborah Kerr and Burt Lancaster in *From Here to Eternity* but in reality the slimy seaweed in my hair and the sand in my mouth and ears detracted from the cinematic moment.

We returned to the picnic blanket to dry off in the sun. I towelled my hair and removed the worst of the sand and laid down beside him. Every cell in my body felt alive. The warm sun inflamed each spot it touched while the breeze did little to cool its influence. He took me in his arms again and kissed me exploringly. He tasted so familiar yet felt so different. I felt I was straddling two time zones. My body was responding to him like it had when we first met while my brain was trying to interrupt and introduce a voice of caution. I longed to feel the weight of his body on mine and my body was about to capitulate to my head when we were interrupted.

A large brown and white and very boisterous dog was bounding towards us. It made a beeline for Christian and leapt excitedly onto the rug scattering clothes and food scraps everywhere. Its long pink tongue licked lovingly up his face and then it plonked itself down between us. I had heard of companion dogs but this one seemed to be some sort of prophylactic one. Before I could even utter a cry of surprise I heard a whistle in the distance and Christian exclaimed, "Max! What the fuck are you doing here?" I looked off into the direction of the whistle and saw a young couple strolling hand in hand along the sand. Christian's gaze followed mine and he sat up hurriedly handed me my shirt and shorts and said,

"Quick, get dressed. This is my dog Max and that," he said pointing at the young couple in the distance, "is Michael and Madeline."

And suddenly Michael and the goddess had assumed the role of parents and once again I was feeling like a naughty child.

12

MICHAEL HAD IT ALL PLANNED. Any lingering doubts he'd had were squashed last night after dinner at Ben's. Madeline had been a huge success as he knew she would be. She had captivated everyone she spoke too even his female friends had made the time to tell him that they liked her. Men were invariably attracted by her beauty and French accent but sometimes women were intimidated by the very same thing. Ben had recounted endless embarrassing stories of Michael's boyhood misdemeanours and she had laughed and teased him about them. Ben had taken him aside late into the evening and said, "This one's a keeper Michael. Don't stuff it up."

He intended to follow his advice. He had his grandmother's ruby and diamond engagement ring in his jeans pocket and he kept nervously checking that it was still there. He had the proposal spot picked out. There was a beautiful bay up ahead which was usually secluded and a cave nearby that he had always considered romantic because of the interplay of light and shade which surrounded it. In his backpack he had two piccolos of champagne. He intended to kneel in the sand, ask her to be his wife and place the antique ring on her finger. He had told no one of his plans in case she said no but he was confident that she loved him and hopeful that she would say yes. He was nervous and distracted though and was not keeping a close eye on Max who had inveigled himself into this outing. So when Max raced off into the distance he assumed it was in pursuit of a seagull.

When he looked up and saw him heading towards some poor couple in the sand he was both annoyed that his secluded spot was already occupied and surprised by Max's behaviour. Max, although a friendly dog was normally well mannered with strangers. He was dreading the apologies he would need to make for ruining what appeared at this distance to have been quite an intimate moment. If he had not been so distracted by his impending proposal he may have realised why Max was not responding when he whistled. It was Madeline who finally said, "Michael, isn't that your father?"

"No, it couldn't be. That man's with a woman." He said without conviction as the man stood up, pushed Max off and waved. "Good God, it is dad."

As he and Madeline drew closer he observed the woman hurriedly cover her bikini with shorts and shirt. Who was she? he wondered. Dad had not mentioned that he was dating anyone but he had seemed a little distracted since they had been here. The woman appeared to be about his father's age. She was a slender brunette with great legs and even though she was sandy and dishevelled he could tell that she was very attractive.

"Dad, Hi! Looks like we will have to send Max back for a refresher course at obedience school." He joked in the hope of lessening the embarrassment.

"Bonjour Chris, it is a beautiful day for the beach n'cest pas? Said Madeline as she smiled warmly at Christian and Julia.

"Yes, yes it is," mumbled Christian. "May I introduce Julia. "

"Julia, this is my son Michael and his girlfriend Madeline. Julia is an old acquaintance of mine on holiday from Australia."

"I'm very pleased to meet you both." Said Julia, as she put out her hand.

"Michael, you look so much like your father at the same age." The resemblance was so striking it unnerved her.

She must indeed be a very old friend thought Michael as he looked enquiringly at his father. They all exchanged a few more awkward pleasantries before Michael and Madeline continued their walk.

Madeline shook Julia's hand and kissed Chris goodbye and as she walked away she wondered about their relationship. There is a something a lot more intense than friendship going on there she thought. She turned around to wave once more and smiled to herself.

"Michael, if you look as hot as your father in boardshorts in twenty years time you will make some woman very happy." She teased and ran ahead.

Michael caught up with her and decided to seize the moment. He grabbed her wrist and spun her towards him and asked,

"Madeline, would you like to be that woman?"

She felt the feather-light touch of his fingers on her wrist and paused to hook her hair, blown by the salty breeze behind her ears. She looked at the nervousness stamped across his familiar face and asked,

"Are you asking me to marry you?" Her heart pounded so rapidly in her slender ribcage she felt breathless.

"Yes, I believe I am." He said as he pulled the ring from his pocket and knelt on one knee in the damp sand.

"Then the answer is yes, oui, I will happily."

He placed the antique ring on her finger and they kissed. Max meanwhile raced giddily around their legs but they were oblivious to his antics.

I helped Christian pack up the picnic hamper in silence and we clambered back to the car. Neither of us spoke until we were sitting in the car once more staring out to sea.

"Well that was awkward," he said, "I'll certainly have some explaining to do."

He did not look at me as he spoke and I tried to imagine why he felt so awkward. He had been divorced for seven years and surely there had been many women in his life since.

"Acquaintance?" I said feeling hurt once again. "I know it was over twenty years ago Christian but I thought you could at least have called me a friend."

"I'm sorry," he said taking my hand once more and after a lengthy pause said,

"Julia, what are you doing here? What are you looking for?" And this time he turned and looked directly into my eyes.

"Is this a philosophical question?" I asked hoping to avoid this conversation.

"You know it's not." He said. "You have suddenly appeared out of the past, turned my life on its ear and started to rekindle feelings I didn't even know I still had. How long are you staying, days, weeks, months? Is it really just chance that brought you to my door?"

I took a deep breath and tried to order my thoughts. I turned my gaze from him and stared back out to sea. I could not think much less answer while looking into those eyes and the emotion they were reflecting. I attempted to explain the conflicting thoughts that had been racing through my head for months.

"When Steve died a large part of me died with him and when Rebecca and Josh left they took another great part with them. I felt like half a person and all that part felt capable of was sadness. I felt that I had forgotten how to be me."

I turned my head to see how he was reacting then continued.

"Then one night a few months ago I sat drowning my sorrows and rereading my old travel diary and I read about you, about how we met, about how I felt, the intensity of our happiness. And as I was reading and reliving, I felt younger; I felt something other than sorrow. In fact I felt like me again. It was like I had rediscovered the essence of me and the feelings we had shared were part of it. Do you understand at all what I mean?" I pleaded.

"I think so. I know that a small part of me died in each of the bad years of my marriage and I felt increasingly diminished. But I must be honest Julia, it scares me that you think I might offer the answer ... I don't have any answers myself and I have never made any woman truly happy."

"Oh Christian, that is not true. You made me happy. I have always been grateful that you were my first love, my first lover. Any woman that had you in her life would be enriched by the experience."

A smile edged slowly across his face and he replied,

"I think that might be the kindest thing anyone has ever said to me but it doesn't answer my question. Tell me Julia, what are you looking for, here, now with me?"

"I'm not sure that I know." I answered truthfully.

"But I know what I am not looking for—I am not hoping for commitment, I've had that—I'm not trying to plan a future. I am just so sick of thinking and analysing. I just want to feel something, to have fun again. I want to react to life for a while without the emotional baggage of the past. I want to take risks ... for one day or many."

I drew my gaze from the comforting ocean and faced him and continued.

"I want to be desired."

"Christian, I know that you are not the fix to my life and it would be unfair to you to expect it ... but I have fun with you. I enjoy your company, your conversation ... your touch. When I am with you I feel like me. I guess I just want to be wanted again ... I want you to want me once more."

I had been brave and honest and I felt naked and vulnerable.

Christian took my hand and brushed it lightly with his lips before he said,

"Julia, I do want you. It scares me how much I do. But I don't think we can just fuck without strings ... there is too much history already between us. Do I explain to Michael that I was in love with you and only married his mother because she was pregnant with him? I am not ready for the complications that commitment brings and although I have had casual affairs in the past I know it wouldn't be casual with you."

I felt like I had been kicked in the teeth. Here I was offering myself naked on a platter and being rejected. In the numerous scenarios that flitted through my imagination before I left home there had been no place for this one. I fought back the tears and said as breezily as I could,

"Fair enough. Could you take me back to the hotel now please."

We reached the hotel and said goodbye like strangers. I reached my room and threw myself on the bed and sobbed. This was supposed to be about fun and lust. How could I have got it so wrong? I understood him not wanting me taking over his life but he didn't even want me in his bed. I would have to pack up and leave. My week's reservation was up tomorrow anyway. I would plan a new itinerary; maybe I could go visit Rebecca now.

I had a long hot shower and washed off the salt and sand. As I rinsed out my swimsuit I thought back to the beach and the passionate kisses we had shared and wondered again why it had gone haywire. Most men offered no strings sex would be queuing up to take a number. But I didn't want most men—I only wanted Christian.

I wrapped myself in the towelling bathrobe, made a minibar gin and tonic and ordered a club sandwich from room service. There was a knock at the door ten minutes later and when I opened it to let the waiter in Christian was standing there still wearing the shorts and T-shirt from this afternoon.

"I'm sorry. I'm an ass." He said. "I got all the way home and then Michael and Madeline announced their engagement and the only person I wanted to share the news with was you. Can you forgive me?"

My eyes welled with tears and I nodded.

"They both thought you were beautiful by the way and sent me to fetch you for a celebration. I guess none of us knows where the future will take us, so I am taking you at your word Julia, if you truly want some uncomplicated fun with a few side benefits," he said and grinned, "I think I can supply that after all."

He kissed my still damp neck and slid his hands inside my robe. My back arched in pleasure and my mouth hungrily sought his when there was a knock at the door again but the club sandwich seemed a lot less appetising now. He pulled my robe closed, tied the sash and said,

"You'd better get that and then get dressed. We are going out for a celebration dinner and, this," he said nibbling my neck again, "will have to wait till later."

My libido was on a roller coaster of desire and denial but I did as I was bid and slipped on my blue silk dress and sapphire earrings and silver bracelet It felt very strange to be dressing in front of a man again but I revelled in his reaction when I let my robe slip from my shoulders to the floor as I made my way to the bathroom.

We drove to Christian's house so he could finally shower and change but not in the yellow Capri this time. This time my carriage was an ageing Volvo station wagon that smelt strongly of dog. Warmth invaded my heart and I said,

"The real you at last?"

"I'm afraid so. Can you cope?" He asked.

"I believe I can," I said as I removed a squeaky dog toy from the front seat.

"Now tell me about the engagement."

When we arrived Christian went to dress and I was left with Max and the happy couple. I was nervous but they both put me at my ease immediately. They were both glowing with love and if possible Madeline looked even more beautiful.

"I love your earrings and bangle," she said, "they are so unusual."

"My daughter designed them. They were a present for my last birthday."

"She has very obvious talent. I don't think I have ever seen anything quite like them. "

"Yes. I think she is talented and each piece she creates is unique. Sometimes people ask her to copy an item but she refuses. She says that jewellery should enhance the personality of the individual wearer so no two pieces should be identical." I explained.

"I can see that she has achieved that," replied Madeline smiling warmly.

"Now tell me about Dad," demanded Michael. "Did you really know him when he was my age?"

"He was even younger than you are now in fact ... but just as cute," I said with a conspiratorial smile at Madeline. "He was wearing flour bag pants when I met him and he was soaking wet. There wasn't much chest hair then but copious amounts of cheek and charm." I said with his photographic image planted firmly in my memory.

"I didn't know Dad had travelled, he has never really talked about it. He sounds so adventurous. It's amazing that you ran into one another again. Fate is such a strange thing isn't it? Tell me, how did you actually meet up again?"

I was thankfully saved from replying by Christian's reappearance, shaved, showered and dressed in dark jeans and a sky blue polo shirt. Watching him alongside his son I could see subtle signs of age that I had not really noted before. He had expression lines of course and small laugh lines around his eyes and there were the first few signs of grey at the temples. His face was more angular than Michael's who still had that fullness in his cheeks, a remnant of his recent boyhood. They both however had that devastating dimple when they smiled.

They were alike in build too, both broad shouldered and long legged although Michael was taller by an inch or two. Michael's eyes were a deep blue and rimmed in dark curly lashes while his father's lashes were quite straight and his eyes as green as pistachios. They walked out the door ahead of us and Madeline linked her arm in mine and said,

"I think I am a very lucky woman," and taking note of the way I was looking at Christian said, "and perhaps you will prove to be also?"

I hope so, I thought as I silenced all the cautionary warnings in my head.

Dinner was in a small French bistro, candlelit and intimate. Conversation and laughter flowed freely until Christian asked Michael, "Have you told your mother yet?"

"I thought we would call on her on our way through London and share the news in person. Madeline is a little nervous. I should never have told her how critical mum can be," said Michael with a rueful glance at Madeline.

"Your mother only wants you to be happy Michael and when she sees that you are she will love Madeline as much as you do." Christian reassured them.

"Do you know Michael's mother, Julia?" Madeline asked.

"No. My acquaintanceship with Christian," I answered looking pointedly at Christian, "was before they met. I don't think I have even seen a photo. What is she like?" I asked with curiosity.

"Blonde and very attractive," replied Christian curtly.

"I think she may have used a few shots of botox to rid her of those constant frown lines though," said Michael grinning at his father.

Christian glared at him but nodded.

"We are going to tell my parents as soon as we return to Paris. They will be ecstatic. They think Michael is simply wonderful. My little sister will be jealous though, she has a small crush on him." She said bumping Michael with her elbow.

Madeline gave me their address and her mobile number and invited me to visit if I came through Paris. "Perhaps I could commission your talented daughter to design a piece of jewellery for my wedding day." She suggested.

"She would probably need your photo and an email address to contact you. But I will certainly ask her if you are serious."

Madeline produced a small digital camera from her purse and took a series of photos of us all. "Will I send copies to your hotel Julia?" She asked.

"No, I'm not sure what I am doing yet. I am only booked in until tomorrow."

"Then I will email them to you Julia and you can choose which ones to send to your talented daughter." Her face was so alight with happiness she was luminescent. I hoped that nothing would ever mar that glow.

"We are leaving tomorrow for Paris Julia and there will be a spare room. You could stay there. It would do dad good to have some company, wouldn't it dad?" Michael brazenly suggested either from innocence or some Machiavellian intent.

I blushed in response, Christian looked embarrassed and Madeline gave me a very knowing smile. Michael and Madeline left to meet up with their friends and Christian and I were left alone. We walked back to the hotel via the beach again and Christian said,

"The moon is still shining on the water, should we make another attempt at that moonlight kiss?"

I checked that my phone was off and that there were no dogs in sight.

"I think we might make the attempt," I said lightly and we kissed, first playfully then with passion until my toes started to curl in the sand. When we finally broke apart he said,

"While Michael is away perhaps you could stay at the house. You would save on hotel bills. I would save on petrol and it would give the neighbours something to talk about. No strings, just fun, just what you requested. What do you think?"

What did I think? Yes, I wanted too. Was it a good idea? Probably not. Was I going to accept? Most definitely.

"You know Christian I've just realised that all our romantic moments have been conducted with our feet in the sand. Do you think it could be a metaphor for our relationship?"

He thought for a moment before replying, "I would worry more if it were our heads."

13

CHRISTIAN COLLECTED JULIA from the hotel the next morning and installed her in the recently vacated spare bedroom. Madeline had put fresh sheets on the bed and a vase of wild flowers on the bedside table. She had also left Julia a note in her elegant handwriting. He was curious as to its contents. It surprised him how well they had bonded in such a short time. He felt somewhat excluded by their easy intimacy.

Max had been despondent when Michael and Madeline had driven off so he turned all his attention now to Julia. She lavished him with affection and he responded with a frenzy of tail wagging. Christian laughed when Julia explained her idea of the prophylactic dog and they decided they should market the idea to parents of teenagers.

He carried her bag to the bedroom and she picked up Madeline's note and read it. She laughed out loud and secreted the envelope into the pocket of her jeans without comment. 'Curiouser' and 'curiouser', he thought. She asked if she might do some washing so he pointed her in the direction of the laundry while he made some lunch. He walked into the laundry to find her on her haunches placing clothes in the gas dryer.

"I have no idea how to work this you know. I asked Max but he is feigning ignorance." She said as she looked up at him. He crouched down beside her and demonstrated the controls. The scene was so mundanely domestic yet so intensely intimate that he would have liked to take her there and then on the laundry floor, but the prophylactic dog was wedging his way between them again.

"I made some lunch," he said offering his hand to help her up.

"The house is stunning Christian. I couldn't really see it last night. I had no idea you could see all the way to the sea. It's like a painting looking out these windows. I love the careful placement of colour, the intermingling of the white and purple, the diosma and lavender contrast so well with the greenery. When I stand back and squint it's like one long patterned bolt of fabric rolling into the ocean but when you look closer you discover the alcoves like secret pockets hidden in the fabric. Who designed it?"

"It's all my own work. I designed it, planted every shrub, built the rock walls. I love it too. It was an escape when things with Rhonda were unbearable. I have never heard it described quite so lyrically though." He explained with pride.

"You are a man of surprising talents Christian or would you prefer me to call you Chris? Everybody else seems to ... I really know so little about you, your life, your marriage. As you said I just appeared out of the past and rode slipshod over your life." She said apologetically.

"Julia, if I didn't want you here you wouldn't be here. Don't think that Michael shamed me into the invitation. And yes, I am Chris these days but I like the fact that you are the only one who calls me Christian."

The phone on the kitchen bench rang and startled them both. Christian answered it and Julia left the room to give him some privacy but as she was leaving she heard him say with exasperation,

"Yes Rhonda, perhaps they should have rung first but they wanted to surprise you with their good news."

I shut the door gently behind me and went to the laundry to retrieve my clothes from the dryer. I loved the aroma of fresh laundry and held a t-shirt to my face to inhale its scent. I folded them quickly and went to my room to unpack. I had no idea how long I would be staying and worried again about the expectations we were putting on one another. I also wondered how long I would be in the spare room. I appreciated the courtesy of my own space but surely he would invite me into his bed. I remembered the way he had slipped his hands into my bathrobe last night at the hotel and thought it would not be long. I patted Madeline's letter and made sure her enclosed gift was safe. Not too long at all I hope. Max had followed me into the room and sat at my feet.

"Tell me Max," I said rubbing his ears, "what is the evil ex-wife really like? Or are you a fan?"

"No, he's not and the cow is just as mean spirited and difficult as ever. Come on I need a walk and a drink. We'll go to the local. It's about time you had a drink in a good Cornish pub and I need to wash the taste of Rhonda out of my mouth."

Christian was in a temper and walked so briskly I struggled to keep up.

"Do you want to talk about it?" I asked tentatively.

"No! I'm sorry I didn't mean to snap but she makes me so mad. She plays the victim so well that she guilts everyone into doing exactly what she wants all the time, every time. Let's just forget about her."

Christian introduced me to a Cornish beer and I sat nursing a half pint while he downed two pints in quick succession. We ate a couple of packs of crisps and he asked sheepishly, "What did Madeline have to say? In the note?"

"Oh, she just wished me a nice stay and left me a small gift." I answered.

Christian raised one eyebrow and looked at me. "I'll show you later," I said.

"Now, how about I cook dinner tonight? I have had so many restaurant meals in the past three weeks I'm craving a home cooked meal, even one I cook myself. How about it? What do you feel like?" I asked.

"I am very easily pleased ... when it comes to food, so I will let you make the decision." His bad mood seemed to lift as a smile tugged reluctantly at the corners of his mouth

We went back to the cottage to pick up the car but I drove to the local Tesco's on my own as the phone rang again just as we were leaving. It had only been a few weeks since I had been behind the wheel of a car but it already felt strange to drive especially through the narrow lanes. Christian's directions were good and I found the supermarket easily.

Supermarkets in other countries are always more interesting than at home. Unfamiliar products, unusual packaging, different fresh produce make it an adventure. I bought more than I needed because of the desire to try everything new and I had no idea what staples Christian might already have. I decided I would cook salt and pepper squid for entrée and I bought some white fish to marinate in coriander, chilli and garlic for the main. I found some bok choy after much difficulty and decided to serve the fish and greens on cellophane noodles. I assumed he liked seafood but I didn't really know. I hoped he wasn't allergic. Some fresh figs, dates and strawberries should round the meal off well, I thought, washed down with a couple of bottles of good Australian whites. I was in a bicoastal mood so went for a Margaret River Sauvignon Blanc and a Hunter Semillon.

I got lost going back. I had never been good at reversing directions and took a number of wrong turns. I was just doing another u-turn when my mobile rang. It was Christian checking that I was okay, the concern in his voice touching. It had been a long time since a man had been concerned about my welfare and it felt good.

Christian had set the kitchen table complete with candles and flowers from the garden. He would make someone a very good wife, I thought. We worked side by side in the kitchen. He made the marinade for the fish with the fresh herbs I had brought while I prepared the squid. The Sauvignon Blanc was crisp and inviting and we sipped as we worked. The meal would only take about fifteen minutes to cook so I prepared a platter of olives and cheese and we moved to the garden to finish our drinks and watch the slowly darkening sky.

It truly was a beautiful garden, around each corner there was a surprising element—a splash of late summer colour, a hidden stone bench, a sandstone sculpture still retaining the heat of the day. Christian told me that he had worked as a landscaper for a time, both designing and implementing his designs. There were many local gardens that apparently bore his artistic touch. He also taught art and garden design at the local technical college but was currently enjoying the summer break. The physical labour explained why he was tanned and in such good shape.

While I was out he had showered and changed into old faded jeans that were soft from repeated washings and fitted his body like a second skin. He was wearing a fine white cotton shirt with the sleeves rolled to show those forearms that had so entranced me the other day. His hair, still slightly damp fell over his forehead when he bent down to pat Max. He had been a good looking boy who had matured into a disarmingly attractive man. The fine lines around his eyes reflected his age but when he smiled and flashed that dimple all I could see was the boy. He sipped his wine and idly stroked Max's velvety fur. I imagined those same gentle fingers stroking my flesh and those lips moist from the wine locked on mine.

Dinner was a success and Christian enjoyed the meal and I had enjoyed cooking for him. He stacked the dishwasher while I made coffee and a fruit plate. The air was cooling outside so we sat on the lounge and listened to music. He rummaged through his CD collection until he found what he was searching for. He popped the CD in the player and said, "Do you remember this?" It was the Skyhooks track *Living in the Seventies* it had been the only record available at Rantua Abang when we met and it was played almost non-stop till it seemed like it was the score to our lives. I was nineteen again and falling in love for the first time. I looked at Christian and smiled and tucked my legs underneath me on the lounge.

"You look like you did when I met you, sitting there like that," he said. We sat each lost in our own thoughts for a while.

"You haven't told me yet what Madeline had to say." He reminded me.

The room appeared to quieten for a moment while I decided whether to share her note with him. His curiosity showed so nakedly on his face I gave in and passed it to him.

He read, Dear Julia, I hope you find the room to your liking but I fear, no I hope you will not be needing it. If that proves to be the case you may need the enclosed. Our friendship may be brief but I felt a connection between us which allows me to wish that you may achieve your heart's desire. With love, Madeline

"I don't understand. What did she enclose?" He asked looking bemused.

I reached into my pocket and handed him Madeline's gift, a string of three condoms.

He blushed and said, "The cheeky blighter," then turned towards me, took my hand grinned and said, "well that should last the first night." My heart leapt into my throat and my legs turned to jelly as I followed him into the bedroom.

14

CHRISTIAN WAS SHOCKED BY MADELINE'S NOTE. She seemed demure and sophisticated and it never occurred to him that she would be thinking about his sex life. He didn't believe he would ever understand women. It amazed him even more that Julia hadn't been offended but had in fact laughed. He was grateful though for he certainly had not given any thought to anything as mundane as condoms. It forced his hand so to speak and it seemed natural to take Julia by the hand and into his bed. The evening had been one of cosy domesticity and it surprised him how much he enjoyed it. No woman since Rhonda had cooked a meal in that kitchen and she always complained she could never stand him underfoot. He had promised Julia no strings sex but with every moment they spent together the ties linking them tightened.

He had watched her all evening, the efficiency with which she prepared the meal, the pleasure she took in the garden, sitting cross-legged on the lounge, every image invoked in him a feeling of both contentment and longing.

He had imagined this moment from his first sight of her in the café but now he felt uncharacteristically nervous. They had fitted together so well once and he longed to recreate that closeness and passion. He led her to his bedroom and they sat on the side of the bed. He could read the desire in her eyes and the apprehension as well. He wanted to inflame one and banish the other.

They sat on the side of the bed and kissed. He kissed her neck and nibbled her ear. He unbuttoned her shirt, unhooked her bra and cupped first one breast and then the other. She helped him slide her jeans to the floor.

"I want to rediscover your body," he whispered, "I used to know it so well."

He sucked on each nipple till they were erect and then worked his way down to her feet. He stroked the delicate instep of her foot and kissed each pedicured toe in turn. He made his way up her legs, admiring and stroking with a feathery touch the strong curve of her calf. He traced with his thumbs the almost invisible fine stretch marks on her hips. He stroked and nibbled the soft flesh of her inner thighs. She was moaning softly and begging him to enter her. He had been hard before they even entered the bedroom so he unrolled the condom and silently thanked his future daughter-in-law.

"Christian please, I need you inside me now," she begged.

"My aim is to please," he said as he glided effortlessly inside her.

It was like coming home for both of them. He glided in and out slowly until she wrapped her long legs around his waist and pushed him in deeper. He increased the tempo until her legs clutched him more strongly and waves of pleasure rippled through her body. He came almost immediately as well and they collapsed spent side by side.

"You're crying," he said with concern.

"No, it's just that mind blowing orgasm leaking out." She reassured.

He kissed her tear stained face and said, "You are beautiful Julia."

This simple expression of tenderness was her undoing, it released a reservoir of emotion. Years of denial, grief, guilt and unfulfilled longing came to the surface like a tidal wave and brought in their wake uncontrollable sobbing. Christian was at a loss but instinct took over and he cradled her like a child till she fell into an exhausted sleep.

I was woken the next morning by the sound of scratching at the bedroom door. Christian was gone and Max was trying to force his way in. I t was already 10.am and I was amazed at how well I had finally slept and how surprisingly refreshed I felt now. I remembered with horror my breakdown of last night and wondered how I could explain it to Christian. His touch had been so tender and the sex so amazing. He had been giving and my need great but at the moment of climax my mind let me down. My body was lost in almost unbearable pleasure while in my mind flashed Steve's face and guilt at being alive just erupted. Fucking without strings was not going to be as easy as I thought.

The scratching grew more insistent so I wrapped the bed-sheet around myself so as not to shock Max who was obviously feeling his failure as a prophylactic companion and opened the bedroom door. Christian followed behind bearing a tray.

He put the tray on the bed and said tentatively, "Good morning, are you alright?"

"Christian, I am so sorry. You must think I am some sort of lunatic. You were so wonderful and it all felt so intense that I think I just lost it. It had been five years since I had been even held by a man. I had forgotten how amazing it is to make love to a man that you … fancy."

I had been about to say "love" I realised with a shock.

"That's good. I was worried my technique must have been really off." He said as he put marmalade on a piece of toast and handed it to me. We drank our tea in bed with Max trying to worm his way between us while looking longingly at the toast.

"You know we could test that technique again, just to make sure it doesn't need any fine tuning." I said hopefully. "Promise I won't cry."

Christian looked pleasurably surprised and lured Max from the bed with the promise of the last piece of toast. He shut the door firmly behind him, turned to me and said,

"Are you sure Julia?"

"Completely. This time it is just about fun. I feel the need to get a better look at that tattoo." Which I did and a lot more besides and it was fun and I kept my promise. Perhaps my ghosts had been exorcised at last.

15

REBECCA HAD SETTLED INTO the routine of an American college well. It was very different from her university experience at home. She had completed her undergraduate degree while living at home with her mother and brother and had worked part time in a restaurant to help support herself and provide art supplies. She had socialised with university friends but had also kept up relationships with friends from school. American students however moved away from home to attend college and she found it surprising that many never went back. Living on campus had its pluses, the absence of travel time and the camaraderie of her fellow students but she missed a sense of personal space and the opportunity to cook for herself. Sometimes she was overcome by a restlessness for solitude.

She enjoyed her lectures and the challenge of the workshops enormously. She hoped to develop her burgeoning skills as a sculptor and was learning new techniques. At home she had experimented with soft stone sculpture purely for fun but had deemed it 'not real sculpture' because of its accessibility to anyone. Her favourite professor though castigated her for her attitude and accused her of being elitist. He had told her the artistic merit of a technique should not be judged by its simplicity but by what she could create out of this simplicity and she was enjoying the challenge.

She was still creating her unique jewellery pieces as well and longed for the day when she could afford more expensive precious gems and metals. For her semester final piece she had created a bracelet and necklace of the finest silver inset with red coral crafted to resemble a trailing spray of petrified coral. She had called it "The Gorgon's Squint (Flowers turned to stone)" as a tribute to the Kenneth Slessor poem 'Captain Cook'. She was determined to stay firmly in touch with her Australian roots. The creative impetus for this particular piece had been a show on the Discovery Channel about the Barrier Reef. She remembered how fascinated she had been when she first saw the Barrier Reef and its underwater garden.

Her father had taken her snorkelling and she had lost herself in this other world of vibrant colour. She had felt as if she were floating through a painting. It had been the last holiday they had before his diagnosis. It was almost five years now since his death and she still missed him, not with that same intensity but more as a longing to share her thoughts with him. She wished she could email him they way she did her mother.

Rebecca was missing her mother greatly and when Pete cheated on her she longed for her mother's warm consoling embrace. She knew she was an adult and could have got through her anger and hurt but was grateful that at least she could talk to her. Her mother had taken on the role of both parents after her father died and had continued to create for her and Josh a warm nurturing home. She and Josh had both worried that when they left home she would be terribly lonely and the house too large and empty so they were relieved that she had decided to spend some time travelling. She is still an attractive woman, thought Rebecca, it would be nice for her to have an older man to wine and dine her occasionally. And I have just the man in mind, she thought. Hopefully by the time Mum comes to my exhibition I will have everything in place.

Rebecca looked at her watch and realised that she would have to race to catch her next lecture at the far end of the campus.

She raced out the door and straight into the arms of Professor Stevens.

"Oops, sorry professor. I was hoping to catch you, do you mind if I walk with you?"

"It would be a pleasure Rebecca. How is your final piece coming along?"

"Very well professor, "Gorgon's Squint" is complete and I am almost happy with my sculpture but I am just not sure if it is finished."

"Try closing your eyes and running your hands over it, sometimes touch alone can give you the answer." He suggested.

Rebecca looked at his hands as he spoke and the artist in her admired their form. He had long elegant fingers and short neatly filed nails. She could see a few dark hairs curling at the wrists and peeking out through his rolled cuffs. He was only a little taller than Rebecca, at 5ft 9in and stocky with a good head of dark hair. He had many admirers among the female students who appreciated his straight white teeth and the way his eyes crinkled when he smiled. He was wearing his trade mark uniform of black roll neck sweater and cord trousers. His recent divorce had been the subject of much excited conjecture among both female students and staff.

"Will you have any guests at the exhibition Rebecca? I imagine it would be too far for your parents to come."

"My father passed a few years ago but my brother is coming and my mother is flying over from England. Will you be attending the opening yourself professor?"

"I wouldn't miss it. I take great pride in showcasing the work of talented artists such as yourself." He said smiling and she understood why so many women found him attractive.

As Rebecca skipped off to her lecture Robert Stevens watched her pick up the pace and admired her grace. He liked teaching foreign students as they bought a different perspective to class discussion and he particularly liked this Australian student. She was sassy, had an independent outlook and was prodigiously talented but unaware of it. He hoped he would have the chance to discuss her future with the mother. He wondered also if the mother was as attractive as this vibrant young woman.

He was aware of the conjecture about his divorce among the staff but it was an ordinary story, he thought, just two people who grew apart and amicably decided to pursue separate lives. He did not feel scarred by the experience and did not need the many shoulders to cry on that had been offered to him. He had tenure at the college and had meticulously avoided any romantic involvement with students or staff and he intended to keep it that way even now his divorce was final. He liked intelligent women but was bored by academics. However at only fifty he was not ready to give up on the search for an attractive woman to complement his life.

16

CHRISTIAN FULFILLED THE ROLE OF TOUR GUIDE and for the remainder of the week he took me to Cornwall's most picturesque spots. We had picnics and pub lunches in century old buildings and on the few hot days we swam in the gradually cooling ocean. We supermarket shopped together and took it in turn to cook. We went on long rambling walks accompanied by the ever faithful Max who had totally given up on his prophylactic calling. And we made love, passionately, sweetly, languidly, whichever way the mood took us. I traced the mandala on his hip with my fingers so many times that I could picture it in my mind and reproduce it by heart. It was called Luna, Christian told me and was a microcosm of the universe bathed in moonlight. Christian had a fascination with all things Hindu and spiritual. He loved the intricate designs of mandalas and had created many of his own and had even painted a series of four which hung on his bedroom wall.

He took me to see the shop space he intended to convert into a gallery. It was near the café where we had our reunion and only a street away from Barbara Hepworth's Sculpture Garden and I took these to be two very good omens for its success. He had already engaged a builder to undertake the minor alterations required and he even sought my input.

He intended to run the gallery as a co-operative to provide opportunity to other local artists and some of his more talented tech students. He planned to feature two or three different artists each month on a rotating basis and the featured artists would help to man the gallery during their exhibits. In this way Christian would not have to be present at the gallery all the time and would still have time to devote to his own painting and his teaching.

There were many galleries and gift shops in St. Ives and Christian was trying to create a point of difference between his gallery and the others. We were sitting by the ocean one evening with our feet in the sand yet again when I suggested,

"Seascapes, Christian, nothing but seascapes, the ocean in all its glory, stormy, calm, threatening. What do you think?"

He hesitated a moment before answering, "I've been thinking along the same lines myself but every gallery here offers seaside views."

"I know, but they are views not scapes, there are so many sunny beachside paintings but few ones that really show the coastline the way it is. The places you have shown me have been beautiful not pretty; they have been dramatic, windswept and interesting." I argued fervently while tossing an idea around in my head.

"I've got a name for you. How does *Windswept and Interesting* appeal to you?"

He thought for a moment and answered as a grin erupted across his face,

"I like it. I like it very much. We make a good team don't we ... creatively I mean?"

A heavy silence enveloped us as we put back our blinkers and pretended to ignore the implications of his remark.

We had both been following the script I had laid down two weeks ago. It was to be no commitment, nothing but fun and I was certainly having fun in bed and out. We used the L word frequently,

'I love the curve of your back, I love it when you touch me there, I love the way your hair flops onto your forehead, I love your cooking'. But we did not say 'I love you;' we did not talk about the future; he did not ask when I was leaving. We lived for now and pretended tomorrow did not exist. This was what I had wanted.

We set off for home in silence—no not home, I told myself, it's Christian's home; your home is on the other side of the world. Talking about the gallery had unleashed a tide of creative ideas in me and I found it impossible to be quiet any longer.

"You could have different walls for the real art and the more affordable works of your students. They could paint souvenirs for tourists, something better than the mass produced crap in other shops."

"Yes Julia, I'll think about it." He answered patiently.

"You could have wonderful bits of driftwood on the floor or on pedestals." I suggested.

"Yes Julia, I'll think about that too."

"It wouldn't just have to be Cornish seascapes, you could have images of the ocean from all around the globe. You could exhibit some of your Bali paintings—you know the one of the Indian Ocean at Tanah Lot?"

"Have you finished yet?" He asked with a hint of exasperation.

"Not quite. What about jewellery, all related to the sea. You could display pearl and coral pendants or polished stones from the beach. They could be displayed draped across the driftwood or falling out of giant cowrie- shells ... I think I'm finished now."

"Julia, repeat after me, 'Christian is opening a gallery and he thought of it all by himself before I arrived uninvited on his doorstep.'" He instructed.

I did as I was told and although I knew he was joking I was also aware that I was starting to cross the line. It was his life not mine and our golden time of spontaneity and passion could not last forever. But it could last at least one more night I hoped and I was sure I could help it along.

"I'm still not sure I have that mandala committed to memory," I said as I produced pencil and paper, "I think I'll need another very close look."

He slapped me playfully on the bum and said,

"You're a very naughty girl Julia Kennedy ... one more look before I test you on it then, okay?"

I loved his body so much, his long legs covered in golden hairs, his muscular thighs, his broad shoulders and the shadowed V at his hips. I loved to rest my head on his chest and feel his heart beat in rhythm with my own. I loved to feel his warm breath like a touch on my neck as we spooned. I loved his gentle artistic hands with their long fingers and the perfect half-moons on his nails. I loved that he let me warm my cold feet on his back without complaint and never pulled the doona from me when I grabbed more than my fair share. I loved everything about him I thought, except perhaps for the way he jumped any time that Rhonda rang, even after seven years of separation he still always took her call. Even now, even when we were in bed, even when I was busy examining that tattoo he still took her call.

"Darling, sorry to disturb you, what were you doing?" I was not leaving the bed to give him privacy this time.

"Nothing Rhonda, just having an early night. What did you want?" He asked tiredly.

"I think we should throw an engagement party for Michael and Madeline. My home is too small and most of his friends are there anyway so it will have to be at our place ... sorry your place." She demanded with her usual arrogance.

"Rhonda, I am extremely busy with the gallery opening I don't have time to plan and host a party; perhaps after Christmas would be better."

"I thought you would put your own selfish desires ahead of the welfare of your son so I have already organised a contingency plan. I will do it all, all the organising, catering, flowers, the lot. You can pay for it of course."

"Rhonda, I don't know, it really doesn't suit me at the moment. I am tied up with something else." He said as he smiled and ran his fingers down my arm.

"Chris, I have already sent out invitations to Madeline's parents. What will they think of Michael if his father is too busy and selfish to merely provide a venue for a party for his only son?" She argued.

"Okay," he sighed, "when is the party?"

"Four weeks from Saturday. I assume that meets with your hard won approval? When is this gallery of yours opening anyway?"

"The week after the party it seems." He answered with resignation.

"And does this, yet another gallery in Penzance, have a name?" She queried with the disdain obvious in her voice.

"*Windswept and Interesting*," he replied looking at me and smiling apologetically enough to melt my heart.

"How quaint!" she replied, managing to be both insulting and dismissive.

"I will need at least two weeks there to organise everything so I will see you in a fortnight. Don't bother moving out of the master bedroom I will make do with the guest bedroom. Goodbye Chris."

"Rhonda, Rhonda, wait on, you can't move . . ." But she had already hung up.

"Fuck, fuck, fuck! She does it to me every time." He said, slamming down the phone.

No sooner was the phone back in the cradle than it rang again and Christian picked it up quickly and said,

"Look Rhonda you can't just . . ."

"Oh! I guess mum has already rung then Dad? I'm really sorry. She just steam -rollered us into it. I hope you said no!" Michael was sheepish and embarrassed.

"It's okay Michael. I would love to help you celebrate your engagement. Perhaps you could stay on for the gallery opening as well." He suggested hopefully.

"If we can that would be great. Dad ... have you told mum about Julia ... will she still be there?" Michael asked with some trepidation.

"I don't know yet, so, no I haven't. I didn't want to muddy the waters if it didn't prove necessary."

So what was I—the dirt ready to muddy the pristine waters of Christian's life? Not the most flattering thing that I had ever been called.

"Madeline said to tell Julia that she has been in contact with her daughter, who she already loves and they are working on some designs together. And she wants to know if Julia liked the gift." Michael relayed.

"I'll pass that on and tell Madeline that I believe she put it to good use. Good night and love to my future daughter-in-law. See you in a few weeks." Christian hung up and the phone stayed silent till morning.

We sat at the kitchen bench next morning drinking our tea, eating boiled eggs and sharing the morning paper. The sun was streaming in and warming everything bar the atmosphere. We had yet to discuss the phone calls of last night. I knew it wasn't my place to bring it up but it didn't appear as if Christian was going to broach the subject any time soon.

"I think I heard most of both ends of those calls last night," I said tentatively, "Rhonda is moving in is she? You don't need to worry, I will move out. After all I wouldn't want to upset the woman you divorced, the woman who constantly cheated on you."

I tried to keep the bitterness from my voice but judging from Christian's reaction I was not successful.

"Please Julia, don't be like that. You don't understand what she is like. She has history with you even if you don't know about it. It would really hurt her if she knew you were living here." He said pleadingly as he took my left hand and looked pointedly at the wedding ring I still wore. We all have a past we hang on to and for all sorts of reasons."

I couldn't argue with him, he was right so I asked,

"What history Christian? I've never even met the woman."

"When Rhonda and I met I was still in love with you but she was here and you weren't. She knew that I had plans to return to Australia but pregnancy put paid to all that. I tried to love her and I succeeded for a while but she always knew that I had loved someone else more. It ate at her insecurities and when she discovered your old letters at mum's house it confirmed all her fears. I had once loved someone else passionately and completely." He took a sip of his tea, absentmindedly crumbled the toast on his plate, then continued. "She burnt your letters you know and kept the ashes to remind her of what she thought she should have had and never did. I tried to reassure her that it was all in the past, as it was, but she was irrational and felt cheated. And I never admitted it to her but she was right ... I never loved her enough. If she sees you now she will leap to the conclusion that we have been having a relationship for years and she will take it out on Michael. I don't want my inability to love his mother to ruin his engagement or wedding."

I could feel tears welling in my eyes. I did not think it was possible but I did feel sorry for the young Rhonda who felt so unloved. I felt sorry for Christian who was still trying to remedy a situation that was unfixable and I felt sorry for me for I now realised that my wonderful lover had a fatal flaw. He would always take the path of least resistance where Rhonda was concerned. He would put up a fight and would even think he was doing what she wanted reluctantly but nonetheless he would do it. Time after time, ad infinitum. I couldn't judge him for he was right. He had not invited me back into his life; I had just appeared as a fait accompli and for selfish reasons of my own. Although I had denied it to him I had looked upon him as a quick fix.

He was the drug I yearned for to jolt me back into the world of the living again; the drug that reignited my libido. He was the fix to my maudlin introspection. Well, it looked as if I would be forced into detox very soon and like all true addicts I wanted to go out with one long bender. I had two weeks of sex, drugs and rock and roll ahead. Well, two weeks of sex and fun at least and maybe a bit of Skyhooks.

17

CHRISTIAN LOOKED AT JULIA beside him at the breakfast bar and half feared and half hoped she would say something about last night. She cracked the top off her egg and started to chew on her bottom lip, a sure sign that she was worrying about something. He remembered her doing it when they first met whenever she was attempting to formulate a question or comment that she feared might upset someone. He found it endearing then and now. She looks so vulnerable, he thought, with bed hair and a face free from make-up and her freckles shining through. The last two weeks had been perfect. It had been like a continuation of their Bali travels just twenty-five years later. The sex had been a reawakening for both of them and after the first night of frightening intensity she had been true to her promise and it had been fun without tears. He continually hoped that he was wrong and that you could fuck without strings.

After that first time he had not asked Julia again when she was leaving and she had not brought it up either but the question hovered constantly on the periphery of his thoughts. He felt they were living on borrowed time and he would soon have to repay his debt. How could he explain to Julia about Rhonda? He didn't really understand it himself. He knew he was wrong to take her calls, to accede to her will so frequently but it had become a hard habit to break. He would not tell Julia of Rhonda's suicide attempts; the first when she discovered his old love letters when Michael was still young and the last three years ago at the break up of yet another relationship. He had sworn that he would protect her privacy, even Michael did not know.

How did he explain her uncanny ability to appear on the scene any time he showed more than a passing interest in a woman? He knew her behaviour was pathological and she needed help but she tried out therapists like she tried on shoes—one after the other but never finding the right fit. He did not want her to suffer a meltdown now with the engagement just announced so he gave in to her demands once more. Rhonda had so soured him about love and relationships that he had almost forgotten how good it could be.

Julia meanwhile had introduced him to an almost effortless relationship. She was generous and passionate and encouraging. She made him trust himself. Her enthusiasm for the gallery strengthened his belief in its possible success and he wanted her by his side at the opening. So why was he sabotaging it all now? Did he really think he could hide her in the wardrobe for two weeks than bring her back out, dust her off and hope things could resume as blissfully as before? He had to try and explain and find out when or did he hope if, she was going. He stumbled through his poor explanation of the hold Rhonda had on his life and ploughed right in to the next difficult question.

"We keep ignoring it but it won't go away Julia, what are your plans, when are you leaving?"

"Before Rhonda gets here apparently." She answered brusquely.

He looked at her with a hang dog expression and she answered the unspoken accusation.

"Yes, I'm being unfair I know. I keep putting the decision into the too hard basket. I had hoped the perfect plan would reveal itself to me in a moment of divine inspiration but you keep making love to me and then I can think of nothing but the present."

She looked at him hoping he would smile and he did.

"I received an email from Rebecca yesterday," she continued,

"about her show. It's in two week's time and I hoped I could fly over to see it and spend a week with her and Josh then make it back in time for your gallery opening. And that is as far as my thoughts would allow me to travel without input from you."

She looked at him unsurely, not certain of the response she wanted.

"I want you here for the opening too, you are my talisman for success you know." He said squeezing her hand and then after some thought suggested,

"Perhaps what we need to do is just plan in small manageable increments; first increment, managing the ex from hell; second increment your trip to New York to see your son and daughter. Does that sound like a doable short-term plan?"

Christian asked hopefully. Julia nodded her head in agreement.

"So that gives us fourteen days for you to help me choose the works to display and possibly find some really great pieces of driftwood." He said with a grin. "Are you up for the challenge?"

"I'm up for whatever you are offering Christian." She replied rising to her feet and starting to clear away the breakfast dishes.

"Well if that's the case leave those and help me make the bed instead."

So once more he took her hand and led her to the bedroom and all their worries disappeared for an hour.

Christian had already selected a number of his own canvasses for display but he had been inspired by Julia's enthusiasm and creative vision and he wanted to paint something just for her. He began to spend four hours a day on his own in his studio with the door locked. He was painting the scene still so vivid in his mind of the beach at Rantua Abang bathed in moonlight. He wanted to convey the immense beauty of the lumbering giant turtles. He wanted to capture the eerie quiet that felt like the universe at peace. He wanted it to speak to her and tell her what he was unable to put into words. He wanted to unveil it at the opening and present her with it as a gift, a gift that spoke of the love he had felt for her and knew that he still felt.

Julia helped him select the best seascapes that represented the changing moods of the ocean from the artists that wished to exhibit.

His students, at her suggestion were painting smaller more affordable canvases and they were as excited as he was. Julia with her graphic design background had designed flyers and invitations and had promised to help create a web page for the gallery when she returned. There was a buzz of energy surrounding them and it swept everyone along in its path.

Merilyn had offered to cater the opening and he and Julia had selected a menu of finger food for the night. Julia insisted patriotically that Australian wines be served and they felt morally obligated to sample every choice before inflicting it on others. Rhonda continued to ring every day with some new request or complaint and Christian continued to take her calls. They were counting down the days till Rhonda arrived and Julia left.

Christian felt almost as if they were living in wartime enjoying his last leave before their inevitable separation. Time spent with Rhonda was certainly like living in a war zone he thought. He was pleased that Julia was going to see her children. He knew how much she missed them. He had not yet asked her if she had talked to them about him but he was curious to know and would ask her before she left. He did not know whether it was because she was leaving that every moment they spent together was intensified or whether it was just the excitement of the rapidly approaching gallery opening but he felt on fire, like he was finally in synch with the universe. He thought if he could just get through Rhonda's visit and the party without any drama perhaps his life would enter a new era of fulfilment.

Rebecca was very excited about my visit and her chance to show me her new work. I think she was as excited about her exhibition as Christian was about his. She had booked a room for me in a hotel not far from the college and had organised for Josh to stay on campus for a few days so they could spend as much time together as possible.

This was the longest they had ever been apart and they both admitted to feeling a little less than whole. The twin bond had sustained them in hard times but conversely it made their separations more difficult. They had their own lives and different circles of friends but they needed the nourishment of contact to truly thrive. Well- meaning friends and acquaintances had predicted at their birth that they would not be as close as identical twins but it did not appear to be the case. From the moment they were born they sought one another's touch and company; they were almost eight years old before they would sleep apart and even then if either one was upset or sad I would find them asleep side by side, their gangly limbs locked together. They shared clothes through Rebecca's tomboy phase and from earliest times confided in each other about their love lives. To my knowledge neither had dated someone the other didn't vet first until now that is. I doubt if Pete would have passed muster with Josh; perhaps their sense of judgement was impaired when they were apart.

As my departure loomed closer my maternal feelings went into overdrive. I was starting to switch from lover to mother in preparation for the loss of Christian in my bed. The last week spent with him was a heightened experience; every mundane action from shopping for food to doing the laundry seemed imbued with greater meaning. I felt I was in a French film noir that had little dialogue but long and lingering looks full of hidden significance. If I was a spectator I would be shouting for the protagonists to get over themselves and advance the plot but it felt different from the inside out. I knew I was only going for a couple of weeks and would be back for the gallery opening but I had a sense of dread about Rhonda's visit. The hold she had over Christian was illogical and disturbing. I did not want this golden time to end but as Buddha said 'nothing is constant other than change' and I convinced myself that I was ready to embrace the changes ahead.

18

IT WAS OVER SIX WEEKS since I had left my home and the kind ministrations of my hairdresser. My roots needed a touch up and a few more highlights would brighten the face that stared back at me in the mirror so I made an appointment for the morning of my departure. I had a flight from Newquay that took me to Gatwick airport in time for my transfer to Heathrow and my evening flight to JFK. My bags were packed and stowed in Christian's car; he was at the gallery and would pick me up when I was finished and drop me at the airport. I had painstakingly and with much regret removed all traces of my presence at his house so the neurotic ex would not be challenged by the thought of another woman with the man she had deserted. Christian and I had not exactly been discreet and I had met a number of his friends. People were used to seeing us together, shopping, holding hands, visiting the gallery and I felt certain that at least one person would comment on my absence, hopefully in Rhonda's presence I thought spitefully.

I was seated at the basin ready to have my colour removed when an attractive blonde walked into the salon. She was petite and slim dressed in dark jeans and a black cashmere sweater. She wore her hair in a French twist and looked casually elegant. She asked the receptionist to be fitted in and flashed a smile that did not quite reach her eyes.

She had beautiful light blue eyes though that looked eerily familiar. I knew I had never met her so it puzzled me. I was enjoying the scalp massage which is the best part of any trip to the hairdresser and my mind was wandering when the other face I was trying to remember popped into my head. Michael has those eyes, I realised, but his were warmer, very much warmer. My worst fears were confirmed when I heard the blonde telling her stylist that she was organising an engagement party for her son. It was difficult to hear all her conversation with the noise of the blow-dryer but the snippets I caught conveyed more information than I was ready to receive.

"My son has recently become engaged to an absolutely stunning French girl," she said loudly, "and his father invited me down to host the party. He felt incapable of doing it on his own; he has great difficulty doing anything without my help actually." She said smirking. "He insisted that I stay with him, even though we are divorced. Between you and me I believe he is trying to reconcile. I think he wants to present a united front at the wedding next year." She sat quietly for a while in obvious thought. "You know, I may even grant him his wish. He is still an attractive man and I may have been a little hasty in trading him in." She said laughing mirthlessly. I caught her eyes in the mirror for a brief moment and was chilled by the determination I saw there.

"Julia, are you all right? You have gone so pale, let me get you a glass of water." My stylist rushed around drawing unwanted attention to me.

"No, I am fine really; just the heat from the blower probably. Thankyou, you have done a wonderful job on the highlights I love them." I said as quietly as I could.

I paid for my cut and colour and tipped the stylist generously and sent Christian an sms telling him that I would walk to the gallery and meet him there. I was almost out the door when my stylist said,

"Have a great time in New York with your family Julia." As I reached the street I heard Rhonda say,

"How strange! Is she American? With those freckles I was sure she would have been Australian. I really don't like Australians they are so pushy and common."

I walked the two blocks to the gallery composing myself and rehearsing what I would say to Christian. He came out to meet me smiling and complimented me on the new hairdo. He kissed me, opened the car door and motioned me inside just as his mobile rang. I knew who it would be and watched him carefully to gauge his reaction.

"You're a day early! No, I can't collect you now ... I have business to attend to. Grab a taxi! I'll see you tonight then."

He sighed, flipped his phone shut and said, "Sorry."

Max was in the back seat and greeted me with his typical enthusiasm, at least someone likes Australians.

"I just saw her you know, at the hairdressers. She is very attractive." I said remembering her slim good looks. Christian looked alarmed. "Don't worry I didn't speak to her." I reassured him but then just blurted out,

"Christian, don't trust her; she's not here just for the party. She's planning to win you back."

Christian looked tired and exasperated.

"Julia, I don't care what she wants, what she's planning. I will not be a participant. She will be gone as soon as the party is over. You and I have a date for the opening. Without your input I don't think there would even be a gallery." He reassured.

"Don't you trust me?" He asked.

"I trust your intentions Christian but I'm not as confident about your resolve." I answered. And I certainly don't trust her, I thought.

We reached the airport about half an hour early and decided to grab a coffee inside. Christian went to the back of the car to get my bags and I gave Max a cuddle.

"Max, I am relying on you to take up your prophylactic role again. You have my permission to bite the bitch if she goes anywhere near his bedroom. Okay?"

He licked my hand which I took as a sign of his eager acceptance of the role. If only I had taken the time to teach him how to use email he could have kept me informed.

We grabbed bad coffee in polystyrene cups and sat down to wait for my flight to be called.

"Ring my mobile to let me know that you have arrived safely." He requested.

"I will," I assured. "I was serious about Rhonda though. She really did tell the hairdresser that she wanted you back."

"I'll say it again Julia. I can handle Rhonda all you have to worry about is enjoying the company of Rebecca and Josh. New York will be exciting. Catch some shows, go shopping, go sightseeing, have fun. Remember, one increment at a time."

My flight was called and I stood up to leave. We reached the security gate when Christian asked, "Have you told Rebecca or Josh about me?" I blushed and said, "Not yet."

"Then we both have a past we need to deal with before we can consider a future don't we?" I put my bag on the scanner, kissed him and said goodbye as I walked through the metal detector. I wanted to race back, hug him and say 'I love you' but I didn't. The tentacles of the past still had too strong a stranglehold on the present.

I liked flying but hated the waiting around at airports so I had cut my connection time very fine but luck smiled on me and I made my flight with enough time to be comfortable without time to be bored. I sat next to a young man flying into New York to surprise a girlfriend. They had been separated for six months and he was worried they were drifting apart. Did I think she would be happy that he was arriving on her doorstep unexpectedly and uninvited? The irony, I thought. My only piece of advice was to ring from the airport; surprises are wonderful only when they are not really unexpected and we have time to compose a face that looks suitably yet pleasantly surprised.

I planned to get a cab to the hotel then phone Rebecca to let her know I had arrived so I collected my luggage and made my way through the terminal towards the taxi rank. I was trying to stop my handbag from slipping off my shoulder while wheeling both a small cabin bag and my suitcase. My head was down and I was not looking where I was going so I bumped into a couple who stood in my path. I was annoyed by their intransigence but ready to apologise when I looked up into two identical pairs of blue eyes.

"Gee Bec, I know it's been almost six months but you would think your own mother would recognise you."

"I know Josh, it must be out of sight out of mind."

The wave of love and warmth that welled up inside me was so strong I thought I might explode. I hugged my two beautiful children and tears streamed down my cheeks.

Josh wiped the tears from my face, turned to his sister and said,

"I think she does know us after all Bec."

"Let me look at you just to make sure," I said, "I would not want to accept any changelings into the nest."

No, they were definitely mine but they had changed. Josh's hair was longer and he was sporting the remnants of a tan. There were circles under his eyes and a three day growth on his chin; partying hard or long hours in the studio I wondered. He looked every inch the rock star with sunglasses pushed back on his head. He was wearing a faded black vintage Ramones t-shirt and Converse sneakers and I caught many young women casting furtive glances at his broad shoulders and long denim-clad legs as they strolled past.

Rebecca looked as beautiful as ever and the contrast of her pale skin and dramatically kohl lined eyes was striking. Her tartan dress was short and emphasised her shapely legs encased in black tights and boots. Her blonde hair was pulled to the side and she carried a soft worn leather satchel. She looked like the art student that she was and suddenly less Australian; until she spoke anyway! It was so good to hear Australian accents again. They enveloped me in a hug then bundled me into a taxi.

I had managed to get a really good rate at the Hilton hotel near Times Square which was close to shops, galleries and theatres and Rebecca's hall of residence. They both talked non-stop during the ride, filling me in on all that they had been doing. Josh had arrived yesterday and had already seen around campus and met some of Rebecca's fellow students. Sitting in the back of the taxi between them and listening to their chatter I suddenly felt as though I was home and I had to constantly look out the window at the towering skyscrapers to dispel the feeling.

With my bags dumped in my room we decided to grab some

dinner. It was early morning for me but I did not eat on the plane so was as hungry as they were. We walked to Rosie O'Grady's and settled ourselves in a booth. We all ordered beers and while waiting for our meals they finally asked how I was and what I had been doing.

"You look wonderful mum, sort of relaxed and ... I don't know ... younger," said Josh, "Don't you think so Bec?"

"Yes, you do mum and I love your hair; those copper highlights suit you. You look fitter, more toned. Have you been exercising?"

I choked on my beer as I thought of the sort of exercise I had been doing. When I stopped coughing I managed to say,

"I've been walking along the beach quite a lot."

"Mum, I have been emailing that French woman Madeline about some jewellery she wants me to make. She sounds fascinating; she says she has some very high-powered job in a merchant bank; not what I would have imagined such a beautiful woman doing. She has said some lovely things about you."

"Really? What else did she say?" I asked casually.

"She said you dined with her and her fiancé one night and she admired your birthday bracelet and earrings. She said how much she liked you and something about being introduced by a dog. Dogs in England must be very smart if they are running introduction services."

At this point I should have casually mentioned Christian and our early connection but I couldn't do it. I had this fear that if I told them how I had virtually stalked him they would think that I was not only mad but had also not loved their father. I rationalised that I needed to know where we stood before I burdened my children with this knowledge. So I made a mental apology to Christian and said,

"She and Michael were walking their dog along the beach and it bounded up and knocked me over so they invited me to join them for dinner, along with Michael's father, as a sort of apology. Now tell me about the exhibition." I said hurriedly in the hope of forestalling any further enquiries.

Rebecca's face became even more animated as she talked about her work. It was like watching Christian talk about his art; they shared that same gleam of infectious enthusiasm. I could imagine them enjoying one another's company; I could imagine them liking each other.

"Earth to mum, I said Madeline's fiancé is pretty hot. Did he look as good in the flesh? I wouldn't mind if she cloned one of those for me." Rebecca said dreamily.

"Mum you are all flushed again, it must be the jet lag. We must get you home to bed." She said with obvious concern in her voice.

We walked back to the hotel and I was suddenly overcome with tiredness. I kissed them both goodnight and we arranged to meet in the morning. Rebecca was going to take me shopping; it had been a long time since we had shared a morning of retail therapy and I was excited at the prospect. I showered quickly and fell into bed and revelled in the wonderfully crisp hotel sheets. I fell asleep immediately and slept soundly for seven hours and may have slept longer if my mobile had not beeped with an incoming message. I groggily reached for my phone and saw a new message from Christian. I realised with a start that I had forgotten to let him know that I had arrived safely. I had become unused to accounting for my whereabouts and even though he had been in my thoughts through dinner the kids and their conversation crowded out any further thought of him. I felt guilty and even more so when I read his message. *Do I assume you arrived safely or were highjacked by phone stealing terrorists? Hope kids are ok. No shots fired here yet.*

I sent a reply by sms. *Sorry! I fell asleep. R & J are great.* I thought for a moment and added, *keep dodging bullets. Bed feels empty. xxx*

I pressed send and hoped he would forgive my lapse. I was meeting Rebecca and Josh for brunch in an hour so I grabbed a quick shower and sent some emails to Jess and Sophie updating them on my travel details.

19

CHRISTIAN LEFT THE AIRPORT with a sense of dread and a reluctance to go home. Increments, he thought, one step at a time. He had assured Julia that he could deal with anything that Rhonda could throw at him but he felt hollow and intimidated at the thought of the following two weeks. He knew he should have insisted that she find other accommodation but it seemed so petty when there was plenty of room and it was just easier to give in to her demands. He did not believe that Rhonda wanted him back in her life; he had failed to make her happy the first time around and even she was not that big a glutton for punishment; it was just Julia's paranoia. But why she should be so insecure puzzled him. He did not know what the future held for either of them; he just knew that she made him happy in a way no other woman ever had.

He wondered if he would be a different man, a better man if he had always been loved by a woman like her. He envied her happy marriage; he found it hard to imagine twenty odd years of wedded bliss when he had not even managed two. He would get through the next two weeks somehow he thought and then Julia would be back and by his side for the gallery opening and the future would unfold as it may.

By the time he reached home it was raining. There were lights on in the house so he assumed Rhonda was already in residence. He let Max out of the car and watched him race to the front door and wait patiently for him to open it. Christian took a deep breath walked up the path turned his key in the lock and entered his own home with unaccustomed reluctance. He called out to Rhonda and his voice echoed hollowly through the house. Rhonda sauntered out from the kitchen cradling a mug of tea. Max rushed to her to give his customary polite greeting but she forestalled him with a curt,

"No Max. Down! To your bed now."

He slinked off, tail between his legs to his bed in the coat room and settled himself with a loud sigh and an accusing glance at Christian.

Christian had not seen Rhonda for almost twelve months and he had to admit she looked good. She had always been very slim and well groomed and continued to look after herself. Her hair was sleek and shiny and newly styled. Her forehead was unlined and he wondered if Michael had perhaps been right about the botox treatment. Men had always been attracted by her toned lean body and blonde hair but Christian found the lack of softness in both body and nature detracted from her physical appeal.

"You look good Rhonda," he said in the hope of creating an atmosphere of cordiality and cooperation.

Every time Rhonda saw Christian she was surprised at how attractive she still found him. She had watched him walk from the car to the door and was forced to admire his long legged gait and broad shoulders. He seemed unaware of the impact he had on women and that was undoubtedly part of his charm. It was part of the problem too she knew. Every time another woman looked in his direction she felt insecure and jealous. Numerous therapists had explained her promiscuity as her attempt at punishing Christian for his inability to love her in the way she wanted. She had enough self- awareness to recognise that she was addicted to falling in love. The passion and the secrecy of her affairs made her feel loved and alive. She was happy when she was the focus of a man's attention but lost interest when the ordinariness of life and a long term relationship took over. She blamed her lovers for not being able to sustain her interest.

Christian may not believe it but she really had loved him in her own way. She knew she was still attractive but also of an age when finding and attracting a new man was getting more difficult; perhaps it was time to rekindle the good times they had shared especially now that she had to move out of her London flat. It was a bit soon to mention that problem to Christian though.

"You look well too Chris. It's been quite a while hasn't it? I've got all the party details here for you to go over. Perhaps we could order in and go through them." Rhonda hoped that time spent one on one with him discussing the one thing that bound them, their love for Michael, would help him realise that he still cared for her. How could he not she argued? He was always there when she needed him, always did as she wanted. After all she had left him not the other way around. He had always sworn that he had never cheated on her and therefore she reasoned he must still love her and had probably pined for her for many years. For one horrible second she contemplated the thought he had once loved someone else and she was filled with a fear and hatred so intense that it scared her.

Christian had to admit that Rhonda was a superb organiser and he was confident that the party would go off without a hitch. He was spending as many hours as he could in his studio putting finishing touches to the works for the opening. He had finished his painting for Julia and was excited about showing it to her.

She had been gone almost a week now and apart from an initial text message he had not heard from her. He knew she would not ring the house but had expected at least a call or text on his mobile. He was sure she was okay but he admitted to feeling a little hurt by her inattention. Rhonda on the other hand had really been making an effort to be pleasant. She had not snapped at him more than once a day and had even cooked a meal and cleaned the house. Max however remained unconvinced that she was a changed woman and when he wasn't with Christian he kept to his bed.

He and Rhonda had spent a pleasant evening last night looking through old photos and he was surprised to see how happy they looked in the early family portraits. They were looking at a photo of Michael on his first day at the beach and remembering how he had shown a complete lack of fear of the surf when she caught his eye and said,

"It wasn't all bad was it Chris? There were good times."

He looked into her eyes and saw softness and maybe remorse and he felt sorry for her and on an impulse he gently stroked her cheek and said,

"There were many good times, perhaps we didn't value them enough Rhonda."

Rhonda took this small sign of affection as further confirmation of Christian's continuing interest in her. In her mind it was a small step from tenderness to love. She would have no qualms now about putting her plan into action. Christian needed her he just did not know it yet. She felt no guilt now about the text and voice messages she had deleted from his mobile phone. The last few days he had stopped leaving it on the kitchen bench and was constantly checking it for messages; she would not be able to intercept his calls forever. Perhaps it was time for Christian to misplace his mobile.

20

RETAIL THERAPY is wonderful anywhere but retail therapy in New York during sale time with a much loved and missed daughter is Nirvana. Rebecca and I, well fortified by brunch with Josh had the stamina to walk from Times Square to the Garment district, visiting almost every store in Fifth Avenue along the way. She took me to less well known quirky designer stores in side streets. We stocked up on gorgeous underwear in *Victoria's Secret* while at *Macy's* we rummaged through the racks of the ***70% off already reduced prices*** garments and discovered the find of the century, a classic little black dress by Donna Karan that skimmed and hugged in all the right places, was the right size and only $50. I loved American sizing; the psychological boost of wearing a size 4 or 6 is not to be underestimated. Single digit clothing creates a certain glow in the wearer unmatched by the European 40 or the Aussie 10.

We grabbed a quick caffeine boost on the go and headed to *Sephora* for some skincare products and makeup. I felt like a child given free rein in a toy store. Rebecca approached one of the ever helpful sales assistants and asked for her expertise in 'updating' my look. She sat me down on a stool, placed a cape around my shoulders and set to work. She was an artist and my face her blank canvas.

"I think we should try a mineral makeup. It will cover and even out your skintone without being heavy. It's wonderful for photos too as it reflects light."

The assistant explained as she quickly brushed a powder over my face, adding more on features that needed highlighting and less on the areas that didn't, or it could have been the other way around. All I really know is that when she finished I had sculpted cheekbones in my round face. I was a miracle of modern cosmetic science.

"You have beautiful eyes. I would love to create a dramatic evening look that will really feature them." She said as she looked to Rebecca for permission and I felt like both a child and an art work in progress. She applied a line of dark pencil on the inside of my lower eyelash line that in some scientific way known only to make up artists made my eyes look larger. She finished with a smoky eye-shadow and two coats of a lengthening mascara and a warm peachy lipstick with a dab of gloss in the centre of my lips. She passed me a mirror and I was so enamoured of my image I bought every product she recommended. As Rebecca and I walked back to the hotel I kept seeking furtive glances at my reflection in shop windows.

Rebecca left me at Union Square to go to her hall of residence and said as we parted, "Leave your makeup as it is, you look amazing and about five years younger. Are you alright to grab a taxi tonight?"

I assured her I was quite capable of this simple task and promised I would be at the art show by 8p.m. I was so laden with packages that I needed help in opening the door of the hotel and then finding a free hand to press the lift button. I scattered my purchases across the bed and excitedly rediscovered my wonderful finds. I took some photos with my digital camera which I uploaded onto my laptop and sent to Jess with an email. A shopping find always brings greater pleasure when it is shared.

Jess and I had spent countless hours shopping over the years and had often bought the same outfit in different colours and just as often borrowed from each other. I was surprised at how much I missed her. I missed her exuberance and positive take on life. I missed her uncritical acceptance of me but most of all I just missed her company. We had shared so much, fun and sorrow and I trusted her completely yet I had not told her of the purpose of my trip or of the weeks I had spent with Christian. Some part of me felt that if I shared my burgeoning love for Christian with anyone from my other life it would dissipate and be reabsorbed into the ether of the past.

I longed to speak to Christian but when I rang his mobile it went straight to voicemail. I had always hated answering machines and seemed to be struck dumb by the sound of the tone beseeching me to leave my thoughts. I ended the call and promised myself to try again later. I was enjoying New York and my children's company but I felt cut adrift from both my old life and my recent one.

Rebecca had told me to wear my new Donna Karan dress and I needed no persuasion. It was simple and elegant and with new Mary-Jane patent-leather heels and my sapphire and silver jewellery I felt quite sophisticated. My make-up had survived a luxuriant bubble bath and my hair only required a little finger styling to regain its body and sit flatteringly on my shoulders. I checked my image in the full length mirror as I left the room and I looked disconcertingly unlike my usual self; prettier and younger maybe but not really me. My sense of dislocation was increasing and I told myself to stop being so fanciful.

The exhibition hall was striking and very full with guests of all ages and ethnicities. I felt excited that Rebecca was exhibiting in such prestigious surroundings. I checked my coat, grabbed a programme and was handed a glass of champagne. I took a few quick sips for Dutch courage and scanned the gallery for a glimpse of Rebecca or Josh. I must have looked lost for I was approached by an attractive middle-aged man who asked if I needed assistance.

"No, I am fine. I am just looking for my daughter, she is one of the students exhibiting tonight."

A fine pair of dark eyes looked searchingly at my face and I think I blushed for he said,

"I'm sorry for staring. Are you Rebecca Kennedy's mother? There is a strong resemblance and your pendant looks like Rebecca's delicate craftsmanship."

"Yes I am. Have you seen her, she doesn't know I am here yet? I'm Julia Kennedy." I said as I put out my hand and wondered who this man was that knew my daughter so well.

He took my outstretched hand and shook it and held on just a fraction too long as he said,

"I'm Robert Stevens, one of Rebecca's professors. It is a great pleasure to meet you Mrs. Kennedy. I had hoped to see you tonight to discuss Rebecca's future. She is one of my most talented students," he said as he flashed a kilowatt smile that showcased a fine example of American dentistry, "and by far the nicest," he added.

He had a warm and kind face with a strong jaw-line and a luxuriant head of messy dark hair. He was a very good looking man and I was conscious of our conversation drawing attention from a number of women nearby.

"I must not keep you from your daughter. I think you will find her in the other exhibition room. I would really like to catch up later and talk about Rebecca if you have the time."

"What mother rejects an opportunity to hear praise of her child? I would love to Professor."

"Please call me Robert." He entreated.

"Certainly Robert, if you call me Julia." I responded.

How very civilised we were! He took my hand and held it a fraction too long again. I felt him watch me walk across the room as I went in pursuit of Rebecca and I was not sure if I was flattered or intimidated.

Rebecca rushed over and gave me a warm hug and whispered in my ear,

"You look sensational Mum. Did I see you talking to Professor Stevens? He's gorgeous isn't he. He is divorced you know." I thought this an odd piece of information to impart and even more so when I saw her make furtive eye contact with Josh and smile.

"You look beautiful too Bec." She looked stunning in a vintage sixties mini dress in baby pink. Her legs were bare and tanned and seemed to go all the way to her armpits. Her fair hair fell in soft waves half way down her back. Her make up was minimal apart from her signature kohl lined eyes and she looked very happy with a smile that warmed a room. Josh was wearing another variation of rock-star at leisure with a soft tan leather biker jacket that hugged his broad shoulders to good effect.

"You scrub up well mum, hardly middle-aged at all." He said as he grinned at me. He had always had a facility with words!

Rebecca showed me her sculpture. It was an abstract depiction of a mother with her arms wrapped protectively around her child. The lines were smooth and flowing and the angles caught the light to create depth and shadow. It was beautiful and moving and I found tears welling in my eyes. Rebecca handed me a tissue and hugged me again.

"You know that is us don't you? The way you have always been there to protect and comfort." The way the tears were streaming down my face I would soon have no makeup left. I felt so proud of her; of her talent, of the sensitive caring young woman she had become. Her coral and silver jewellery piece was equally stunning and she told me excitedly that a number of people had asked to purchase it. She even had a business card from a Fifth Avenue jeweller who wished to discuss her designs with her with a view to stocking some of her creations. Her skin could barely contain her excitement and she was bouncing on her feet like the child she had not long left behind. She had always bounced when she was excited and every Christmas Eve she was like the ball in a pinball machine deflecting erratically off everything in her path.

Josh and I took a tour of the exhibition and were floored by the quality of the students' work. A stainless steel, many faceted tower took my attention. It reflected the room and its occupants in its many different planes polished to a mirror-like surface. It represented New York very well and made me think of the destruction of 9/11. It was a very confronting piece and brilliantly executed. When I saw that the artist standing beside it was the boy who had broken Rebecca's heart its brilliance dimmed dramatically. When I saw how hard Josh was glaring at him I realised Rebecca had shared her tale of woe with him. Pete was fortunate that he was in a crowd for I feel sure Josh would have provided him with a more lasting reminder of his cheating behaviour.

There was a contemporary painting of the lights of the traffic seen through a rain soaked window that really captured my imagination; up close it was just stripes of thickly applied paint but at a distance you could clearly see the yellow cabs and the flashing traffic lights glimpsed through a drizzle of rain and Venetian blinds. I kept returning to it and while lost in contemplation for about the fourth time I felt an unexpected tap on my arm that caused me to jump.

"I'm sorry Julia, I didn't mean to startle you. Rebecca sent me over to tell you that they are going on to a party."

Robert stood beside me looking somewhat embarrassed and I turned in time to see Rebecca and Josh walk off with a wave and a silently mouthed 'I'll call you tomorrow.' I was a bit miffed that they had not said goodbye and knew that they normally exhibited better manners than that. Robert cleared his throat and said hesitantly,

"I was wondering if I could give you a lift back to your hotel. I go right past the Hilton and it would give us a chance to talk about Rebecca."

How did he know where I was staying? I hesitated in replying and he must have sensed my unspoken question for he said, "Rebecca told me and asked if the hotel happened to be on my way home."

I blushed and apologised awkwardly for the atypical rudeness of my offspring.

"I'm really sorry Robert it is not like Rebecca to be so thoughtless. I will be perfectly fine to get a taxi."

"Julia, please, it would be my pleasure and it seriously is not out of the way."

I accepted as graciously as I could but was still fuming at my daughter. Robert took my arm and we headed to the cloak room to collect our coats. There was now a distinct nip in the air and I gratefully slid into the coat he held out for me. The university had students acting as valets for the evening and when he handed over his ticket I had time for conjecture over what car he would drive. I imagined something sophisticated, sleek and European to complement his elegant intellectual image and my guess was confirmed when a black 3 Series BMW pulled up. I smiled to myself and he looked at me quizzically expecting an explanation. I could think of no way to explain without sounding presumptuous so I remained silent.

We chatted amiably about the art works displayed. He listened intently to my views without condescension and I was struck anew by his warmth and humour. The trip was brief and we had not yet discussed Rebecca so I was not unduly surprised when he suggested coffee in the hotel bar.

We both ordered coffee and liqueurs, a cognac for him and sambuca for me. We talked of Rebecca's educational background and her early interest in all things creative. He surprised me with his accurate insights into her personality garnered after such a short time. His students were certainly fortunate. He both cared and was very pleasant to look at; he was intellectual eye-candy, the jackpot in education.

He asked about her father and I longed to share her triumph with Steve. He had been so proud of both the children and he had nurtured their appreciation of music and fine arts almost from infancy. He had built them easels and finger-painted with them as pre-schoolers and built elaborate sand sculptures on every beach holiday. He had taken them to art galleries and encouraged them to use touch as well as sight in their appreciation of nature, from the velvety smoothness of our cat's fur to the rough texture of a gum tree's bark. I had often thought that Rebecca's love for texture and touch originated in these early experiences. It saddened me that their father had to miss out on seeing his loving input bear fruit.

It was almost 1.am when Robert made a move to go. We had sat in companionable silence while waiting for the bill which I had charged to my room against his protests. He stood to take his leave then hesitated briefly and said,

"I wonder if you would like to accompany me to the faculty Halloween party tomorrow night. I know it is very short notice but it is usually an entertaining affair and you could consider it as an exercise in cultural tourism." He added as he flashed a wry smile. "I understand Halloween is not really celebrated in Australia."

I was unprepared for the invitation. Had Rebecca put him up to it? Perhaps he felt sorry for me alone in a big city. Was it a date? Can I go on a date when I am involved with Christian? I needed to phone a friend or ask the audience but I was forced to make my own snap decision.

"It is very kind of you Robert but I have no costume to wear ... and I am sort of involved with someone at the moment." A quick look of disappointment flashed across his expressive face so I added, "I have enjoyed your company immensely but I would not want to spend time with you under false pretensions."

A slow smile crept across his face and he looked at me with a gaze that was as direct as his words.

"Can I be really honest with you Julia?"

"Please." I said nodding.

"I am fairly recently divorced and there seems to be a misguided belief amongst my circle that I must be lonely. I appear to be the victim of a relentless campaign to pair me up with a fellow academic. Some of them can be quite predatory beneath their genteel exteriors." Again there was that wry grin.

"If I go to this function dateless I will be pestered all evening and if I go with a colleague we will became gossip fodder. So would you reconsider Julia? It would not be a date; just two people who I believe enjoy one another's company spending what I am sure could be an enjoyable evening together."

He looked at me with his pleading Spaniel eyes and added, "and you will not be in New York long enough to suffer from the aftermath of the rumour mill."

I was not sure whether to be flattered or insulted but I accepted his invitation and left a note for the concierge to contact me about obtaining a Halloween costume. Strangely enough the faculty function was to be held in the hotel ballroom and I reasoned that if things went awry I could easily disappear to my room.

I longed to hear Christian's voice before I went to sleep and rang his mobile again but once more it went direct to voice mail. This time I was mature enough to leave a brief message telling him I missed him and asking him to call me at anytime. I sent a very short text to Rebecca, *Ring me!* I hoped my displeasure at her presumption was evident in those two words.

I slept but my slumber was disturbed by dreams of Rhonda handcuffing Christian to the bed while Max disguised as a white charger attempted unsuccessfully to come to his rescue.

21

I AWOKE WITH A FEELING of apprehension and regret at my acceptance of Robert's invitation. The thought of smiling crowds and clattering dishes did not appeal this morning so room service seemed a good idea. The tray was delivered with quiet efficiency along with a note from the concierge listing a costume hire place a short cab ride away.

After a long hot shower I felt more able to face the world and the hopefully not too daunting task of choosing a costume. I had checked with the hotel staff to make sure it really was a costume ball. I did not want to be like Brigid Jones and appear in a bunny costume at a soberly dressed function of New York academics.

The streets were shining after a last night's shower and beams of sunlight were fighting their way through the gaps between skyscrapers. I thought again of Pete's metallic sculpture and wished I had not liked it so much. It seemed disloyal to recognise talent in the cheating boy who had mistreated my daughter.

I loved the New York skyline and this surprised me. I had always thought of myself as a wide open spaces kind of person and too long spent in cities usually had me yearning for the mountains or the coast, but New York was unlike any other place. It had an energy that seemed to nourish and a beauty that revealed itself slowly.

The proprietor of the costume shop was as wide as he was tall; he could have painted himself orange and gone to any party as a pumpkin. When I asked what costumes he had he threw his arms in the air flamboyantly and questioned my sanity.

"You do realise it is the day of Halloween and the shelves are almost empty. Why people leave it so late astounds me."

I explained that my invitation had been received late and then felt foolish for trying to justify myself. I was a paying customer after all and they must have something left or they would not be open for business. I drew myself up to my full height which was at least four inches taller than him and said with some aplomb I hoped,

"Do you have any literary costumes? Something from Shakespeare perhaps?"

"No."

"How about an historical figure?" I asked hopefully.

"No. We have some Disney characters left."

I reassessed my options. Snow White or Cinderella would probably be alright.

"No sorry, only children's sizes left in those. I could do Donald Duck or Minnie Mouse." He offered.

Not quite me. I was getting desperate.

"Do you have anything at all to fit an adult woman that is not a cartoon character?"

"We do have our more adult range." He said with a slow smile.

"Adult in what way exactly?" I asked nervously.

"Oh you know, the sexy nurse, schoolgirl, fan dancer type of thing. I'm sure I could find something to fit you in those." He said turning around while his arm stretched to the shelf behind him with eager anticipation.

Yes, I thought and I guarantee you give very attentive fitting help with those. I did not think Robert would be so happy to escort me if I turned up in fishnets wearing nothing but a fan. It might be fun with

Christian though. I must investigate that prospect later.

"Let me restate. Do you have any costume to fit an adult that is not a cartoon character or a facsimile of a porn star?"

"We have our classical line, Greek and Roman costumes just arrived from China. They are for purchase though not hire."

Ancient Greece via China for an Aussie, very United Nations but I am all for multiculturalism so I opted for a Grecian goddess costume of white pleated fabric. It was draped over one shoulder and cinched with a gold cord. It was pre-packaged so I was unable to try it on but he assured me it would fit. His delightful assistant returned from a coffee break carrying the giant Starbucks mug which seemed to be grafted onto the hands of all New Yorkers. She was so effervescent I think she must have been mainlining caffeine. She suggested I wear my hair up in curls with a wreath of golden leaves and carry a bunch of plastic grapes.

"Do you have gold sandals? Super. You're lucky you have a tan. Take some photos and send us one. I haven't seen this costume on yet. Halloween is so exciting. We are shutting just after lunch you are lucky you got here in time. Hope you have a fun time. I know you will, everybody has fun at Halloween."

My brain was finding it difficult to process her rapid fire speech. If she didn't slow down I feared she would combust by dusk. I thanked her for her help and as the package was light I opted to walk back to the hotel. There was more bounce to my step now even without the double espresso.

I had always loved dress-up parties and Steve and I had hosted quite a few over the years. We'd had Hawaiian nights, superhero parties and a particularly memorable roaring twenties night complete with speakeasy gin and old mafia cars. Our Mardi Gras night too went down in local history and the photos of the night can still be used to blackmail friends. There was something about dressing up that loosened inhibitions and removed the awkwardness from conversing with strangers. Hopefully tonight would be such an event and Robert was right, it was an American cultural experience and one I had never experienced.

Rebecca had been suspiciously quiet all day, she knew I was not happy with her so I accepted the olive branch she offered when she phoned and said she would come to my room to help me dress.

I still had not heard back from Christian and was starting to feel anxious. Perhaps he really was chained to the bed. Surely there was some time of the day or night when he was free of Rhonda's ever-seeing eye. I wanted to tell him about the adult costumes; maybe I should turn up at his opening as a naughty schoolgirl. I missed him even more than I thought I would.

Rebecca arrived promptly at six armed with makeup and her curling iron but looking very sheepish.

"What on earth were you thinking? I've never been so embarrassed, conning him in to taking me home! It is just as well that I love you." I said embracing her.

"I thought a little bit of adult company, attractive male adult company, might be good for you. I know you loved dad but it is time to move on. I thought a little holiday romance might get you started." She explained. "After all mum it's only a date. You don't have to sleep with him." She paused for a moment then added, " but if you do I never want to hear about it!"

"Rebecca, for heaven's sake, of course I'm not going to sleep with the man ... why, would you get higher grades if I did?"

"Very funny! Now let's get your hair curled and looking like you just stepped down from Mount Olympus."

Rebecca curled my hair with her usual quiet efficiency and used her skill to transform my face into something more classic than freckled Aussie. We chatted about college and her friends and she told me of the party she and Josh were attending later that night.

"Two of my friends are already fighting over Josh. They love his laid back attitude and he is just lapping up the adulation. Mum, can I ask you a question?"

"Of course honey," I replied with some hesitation.

"Do you think you will ever get over Dad and find somebody else?" I looked at her reflection in the mirror and saw Steve's serious blue eyes staring back at me.

"I won't get over him because I loved him and I see him in you and Josh all the time but I think I am ready to try and move on." I answered honestly.

"I'm glad." She said giving my shoulders a squeeze.

This was a perfect opportunity to talk to her about Christian and I spent some minutes trying to find the right words.

"Actually it's funny that you should bring this up now because ..." I started to explain when the door bell rang.

"That must be Josh. I told him to meet us here and get some photos. Hold that thought Mum, I'll go and let him in."

"Come on Mum, get a move on, your date awaits." Josh instructed.

"It's not a date." I argued as I went into the bathroom to put on my costume. I laced up my sandals and slipped the dress over my head. I had to go braless because it draped over only one shoulder and I had neglected to pack a strapless bra. It felt tight as I wriggled into it and I tried to pull it down to knee length like the picture on the packaging but it was going nowhere near my knees. Maybe in China it was knee length—on me it barely came to mid thigh and although the front draped the back of the dress hugged me like a second skin. I placed the gold wreath on my forehead and the gold cord around my waist. I closed my eyes before I faced the mirror in the hope that the dress would grow another six inches but to no avail. I can't go out like this—it was worse than the adult costumes I'd rejected. There was a knock at the bathroom door and Josh called out,

"Come on Mum. Let's have a look."

I took a deep breath and opened the door. They both looked at me and tried to keep their mirth from showing in their faces.

"Um, where's the rest of it? Still in the packaging perhaps?" Josh said through gales of laughter as he looked through the discarded wrappings.

"Still in China I guess." I said with no option but to join in the hilarity.

"You were right Mum. It will be straight A's for me from now on. Whatever you do don't bend over." Rebecca handed me the bunch of grapes with tears streaming down her face.

"I can't go and show my face like this." I said with desperation.

"Don't worry it's not your face that is showing," said Josh who was by now in convulsions.

"Mum you can't let the professor down and be thankful you have good legs. Have a couple of drinks and you'll be fine but remember . . ."

"Don't bend over!" They chorused together.

My first drink could not come soon enough. They pushed me out the door and even as it shut I could still hear their laughter and the faint echo of a ringing mobile phone.

Robert was waiting for me in the lobby dressed sedately as Sherlock Holmes in a tweed coat complete with deerstalker and pipe. His eyebrows raised in amusement and a smile tugged at the corners of his mouth.

"I deduce my dear Watson," he said turning to an imaginary companion, "that there were not many costume options available at such short notice."

"Your deductions are correct Mr. Holmes. Maybe you should just go on your own." I offered.

"No, this is wonderful Julia, you look amazing. This will certainly get the tongues of academia wagging." He slipped his arm through mine and said,

"Let's enter the fray shall we."

I took a deep breath and held my head high while repeating the mantra, 'do not bend over, do not bend over.'

The ballroom looked breathtaking, jack-o-lanterns adorned every table, cobwebs hung from the ceiling and most importantly waiters hovered nearby with trays of champagne.

I downed one glass very quickly and as the bubbles of alcohol filtered through my bloodstream I started to relax and have fun. There were many literary figures among the costumed guests; King Lear, Macbeth, the Great Gatsby, Heloise and Abelard, Romeo and Juliet along with Catwoman and Batman and one drably dressed woman with an enormous nose carrying a manuscript and a handful of pens. I pointed her out to Robert.

"Who do you think, Virginia Wolf?" I conjectured.

"Probably. She is an English tutor." He agreed.

"I can't believe she even went to the trouble to get a prosthetic nose." I said in admiration.

Robert spluttered into his champagne and almost choked.

"I think you'll find the nose is real."

Oh dear, I guess there are worse things than showing too much leg.

The band was wonderful and played a lot of swing that had everybody who fancied themselves as dancers twirling around the dance floor with abandon. Robert stood by my side as we watched the dancers who exhibited varying degrees of dexterity joining then leaving the dance floor. I could not help my feet tapping to the rhythm and he turned to me and said,

"I'm game if you are."

We edged our way on to the floor and I remembered Josh and Rebecca's advice as we waited for the next song to start. We acquitted ourselves with some flair I thought, sort of round two of *Dancing with the Stars*. Robert moved well and I enjoyed myself immensely. Discretion however dictated that we sit out the rock and roll numbers. I had no skirt to twirl and the more vigorous the dancing became the more my costume rode up my thighs; one more spin and I feared I would be wearing a midriff top.

Robert procured me a plate of supper and we found a quieter corner to sit where we could talk. I wanted to check my phone for messages in the hope that Christian had finally got back to me but I was having difficulty enough balancing plate and glass and it was impossible to reach into the folds of my bag to retrieve my phone as well. I was obviously fidgeting and looking awkward for Robert said,

"Can I help you with something Julia?"

"Sorry, I know it is rude but do you mind if I check my phone for messages. I have been waiting for a particular call for days."

"Here let me hold your glass. Do you want some privacy?"

"No, not at all." My hand rummaged in my bag and I found lipstick, compact and eyeliner but no mobile. I must have left it in the room. "It's not here. I was a bit distracted when I left the room," I said as I looked down at my bare thighs, "and must have left my phone behind."

"I understand the distraction perfectly—those shapely thighs have been distracting me also. Do I assume this call is from the 'someone that you are sort of in a relationship with'?"

"Yes it is." I admitted a little sheepishly.

"Watson tells me I'm a great listener if you feel like talking about it." He offered in his gallant fashion.

My instinct was to say no but I realised with surprise that I did want to talk so I told him the whole tale from the beginning. I told him of how we met twenty odd years ago; I told him of my stalking of Christian; I told him about the ex-wife and Christian's gallery and talent. I talked about everything but the sex. It felt very good to finally share my story and my concerns.

"So, what do you think?"

"I am impressed and scared at the same time. I think you were very brave to take such a chance. I'm not sure how I would have reacted if someone from my past tracked me down. You are a surprising woman Julia."

"Can I ask you something Robert? Do you have hang ups about you ex? Do her needs still dominate your life?" I knew as I asked the question what his answer would be.

"I still care about her of course but we don't love one another anymore. I certainly don't speak to her daily and I would never put her before a woman I was interested in, someone like you Julia." I think I blushed because he looked away.

"Well Mr Holmes do your brilliant powers of deduction enable you to predict whether Christian and I have a future together?"

"If the man doesn't try to keep you he is crazy but he certainly seems to have some serious issues with the ex to work through but," he added soberly as his eyes held my gaze, "if it is as good as you say it is when you are together then it is worth fighting for." There was a lull in the conversation as people started to take their leave and came over to say goodnight,

"There is one thing I would like to add though—you became so animated when you talked of the gallery ... have you ever given thought to setting up a business like that yourself? You have something distinctive and unique to offer in your own right. You obviously have a good critical eye for art and a sound business head. You should go for it. I can see it now *Windswept and even more Interesting*." He said smiling.

"Now you are teasing! It does interest me though. Thankyou for the vote of confidence in my abilities. Who knows what may happen, I may take your advice one day." I said stifling a yawn.

We looked around the ballroom to see very few guests remaining and I was suddenly overcome by weariness. Bed was looking very enticing. Robert escorted me to my door and as I fumbled with the key he said,

"I hope this man of yours knows what he has in you."

"I hope so too. Thankyou Robert for a wonderful evening and it certainly lived up to all my cultural expectations."

He took my hand to shake and I leant in and kissed him lightly on the cheek.

"You are a very sweet man Robert Stevens."

"Just what every middle-aged man longs to hear." He said with a grimace.

"Okay, you are not sweet; you are smart, funny, sexy and devilishly handsome. Is that better?" I asked.

"You forgot to mention what a superlative kisser I am also." He boasted as he surprised me with a kiss that lingered on my lips long after he had gone.

"I wish I had met you earlier Julia. Email me and let me know what happens with your man." He said handing me a card with his contact details. "Remember I am always available for further cultural education; other things too if your man doesn't live up to expectations." He flashed his now familiar smile.

"Goodnight Robert."

"Goodnight Julia."

I closed the door behind me and entertained for one very brief moment taking him up on his offer.

I went straight to the bedside table to check my mobile and room phone for messages. No missed calls. The silence was perplexing, we had parted on good terms with talk of the future and I couldn't understand why Christian was not returning my calls.

I wriggled out my costume and into bed. I will worry about it all in the morning I told myself. I had been asleep for about an hour when my ringing mobile finally pierced my consciousness. I looked through bleary eyes at the sender ID and my heart started to beat faster. Finally.

"Hello Christian." I said sleepily. "It is so good to hear your voice again."

"Is it? How was your date?" His voice lacked its customary warmth and a shiver ran down my spine.

"Sorry? I didn't catch what you said."

"I think you did. I asked how your date went."

"How do you know about it?" Disrupted sleep was making it hard for me to concentrate and I thought this must be some joke of Christian's.

"I rang last night and a female Australian voice answered the phone. I assumed it was you of course but Rebecca explained who she was and told me that you had just left on a date. She had never even heard of me by the way."

What do I explain first—that I was just about to tell her all about him or that it wasn't really a date?

"It wasn't a date really. One of Rebecca's teachers just asked me to a Halloween ball on the spur of the moment because I had never celebrated it before." I explained expecting him to understand.

"That would be Sherlock Holmes would it?" His voice was even colder.

"How on earth could you know that?" I asked feeling even more perplexed, the kids had not even seen Robert in costume.

"Madeline and Michael stayed for the party and as usual she had her laptop glued to her side. Your daughter emailed her a photo from the function. You and Sherlock certainly appeared cosy for a non-date."

What on earth could Bec have been thinking and when had she taken the photo? I was growing more confused and defensive by the minute.

"Great costume by the way, very subtle, you certainly had it all out on display."

"Christian this is ridiculous. It's two in the morning, I haven't heard from you for well over a week and now we are fighting over nothing ... "

"Well you haven't rung me." He accused childishly.

"I have. I've left texts and voice messages on your mobile. You asked me not to ring the house so I wouldn't upset the ex. That going well for you is it?" I was sick of justifying myself and decided to go on the attack too.

"Strange I haven't received them then isn't it?"

"Don't you believe me?"

"I don't know what to believe Julia. I guess I didn't believe that so soon after you left my bed you would be working your way into another. Just stage two of the fucking without strings campaign is it?"

I cradled the phone in my hand and tried to compose myself.

"That's a really horrible thing to even think but to say it is unforgivable. I did not sleep with him. You should know me better than that." I pleaded on the verge of tears.

"Maybe we don't really know one another at all Julia. I only know what you have told me; you could have slept with dozens of men since your husband died. I had a cheating wife once. I won't be suckered again."

"Perhaps we should talk when you are calmer and more reasonable." I suggested.

"I'm quite calm Julia."

And he was. His voice was frighteningly controlled and it chilled me to the core.

"Christian if you are calm then listen to me. I did not sleep with him and it wasn't a date. You must believe me."

"So, no kiss goodnight? His hand never stroked those bare thighs as you danced?" He said with venom.

A memory of the fleeting kiss at the door flooded my brain.

"I have already explained and I don't need to justify myself any further. Can we please move on before we say anything else we will regret … Did the party go well?"

"Yes, it did. Rhonda is a superb organiser. Madeline's family seem like decent people." He voice started to regain some warmth.

"I'm glad it was a success. Dare I ask if Rhonda is leaving now?"

My heart skipped a beat as I awaited his reply.

"She may need to stay a little longer. I'm not really sure yet."

"Where does that leave us then? Is there still an 'us' Christian?" I asked tentatively. I could hear the seconds tick by on the bedside clock, one, two, three, four, five.

"I hope so Julia. We will have to talk later."

"Christian, I've missed you."

There was another long pregnant pause before he finally said so softly I could barely hear him.

"I've missed you too."

I cuddled my pillow and tried without success to go back to sleep. I had never imagined Christian as the jealous type. Steve had always been so trusting. Perhaps we really did not know one another at all. My restlessness forced me up so I checked my email and there was the offending photo; Robert with his arm snugly around my waist while I tried to hold the grapes out of his reach. We were both laughing happily. We had posed for the shot at the entrance to the ballroom and Rebecca or Josh must have snapped it as they left the hotel. There was another message from Bec. *So sorry Mum, I pressed send all by mistake. Unfortunately everyone in my address book has the photo too. Tequila shots are very BAD! Hope you still love me.* ☹

I thought the night could not get any more complicated but it did. There was a message from Jess as well.

> Okay spill the beans you woman of a thousand faces. Who is the mystery man? Very cute by the way and love your costume. Does the three year old want it back yet? Tell all. Love J.

22

*W*ITH EACH CRUEL *and hurtful accusation that spewed lava-like from his mouth Christian's sense of self loathing deepened. He knew Julia had not slept with this professor and had never for a moment considered that she had lied about her celibacy since her husband's death but when he saw her looking happy with another man's arm around her waist he wanted to punish her. It was irrational and unreasonable but the compulsion remained. Guilt about his own behaviour was fuelling his attack and he knew it.*

He had been excited to finally hear her voice or what he thought was her voice and when he realised it was her daughter he fully expected that she would both know who he was and what part he had been playing in her mother's life. He waited for her to say, "So you're the one she has been talking about non stop," not "sorry, Mum has just left on a date." He was disappointed and hurt and like a thwarted child had lashed out. They had shared so much in the last few weeks and through the joking and the light-hearted repartee there had been moments of intensity and connectedness so overwhelming that they scared yet thrilled him. When he recalled the hurt in her voice he hated himself anew. But she had lied about trying to contact him and surely if she really cared she would have found time to at least mention his name to her kids. He dreaded that she may have cheated but if she had he could at least justify his own behaviour. He was confused, angry and guilty and now he was going to have to deal with the consequences; one hurt and angry lover and one ex-wife who had finally found a wedge back into his life. He had been such a fool.

Rhonda walked out of the bedroom with a look that spoke of her elation about last night. The stuck zipper on her dress had been a godsend and Christian's requested assistance, although initially reluctant had cemented her faith in her plans. She felt confident that this woman she had heard hints of would not prove to be a threat and the conversation she had just overheard reinforced her belief. Who would have thought that Christian could be so cruel?

He believed she had no knowledge of his relationship with the Australian woman but a few of the gallery contributors had mentioned her and Madeline also had let slip a remark about 'Julia' when she thought she was out of earshot. But the icing on the cake had to be the emailed photo. She had walked past Madeline as she was checking her emails and saw the photo and she wasted no time in bringing it to Christian's attention, despite Madeline's best effort to shut her laptop. She thought she had achieved it with a well acted degree of innocence.

"Now that looks like a woman who knows how to enjoy herself. What an attractive man. Is this someone you know Christian?"

The tight shocked look on his face spoke more than words. She hated the fact that another woman caused such jealousy but his cruel phone call as a result was well worth her own pangs of discomfort. Men are so easily manipulated she thought happily. But she needed now to insure that there were no tearful reconciliation phone calls. Christian had been unusually protective of his mobile of late but she was confident in her ability to seize the opportunity when it presented itself.

She had enjoyed the engagement party immensely. She knew that she had looked good in her plum coloured sheath dress. It flattered her skin tones and showed off her long lean limbs and had been worth every penny of Christian's money. He would not even notice how she had pad-

ded out the catering bill to cover its cost. She had enjoyed playing hostess and slipped her arm through Christian's enough throughout the night to give the impression to Madeline's relatives that they were still together as they indeed had been later in the night, she thought smugly. It had all been so easy. A few home cooked meals to show that she cared, a few tears when she looked at the happy couple and a dash of reminiscences of happier times. The trips from the bathroom with the towel slipping from her body had helped remind him of what other men still desired.

She had stroked his ego when it was to her advantage and fed his insecurities when it was not. She had read out from the newspaper tales of internet romances that were full of deception and had discussed within his hearing every story she knew of the difficulties of long distance relationships. Deleting messages from his mobile had been simple as he usually placed it on the kitchen bench when he came in. The fact that he believed her ignorant of Julia's existence had made it even simpler. And last night when she had finally enticed him into her bed she used every trick she knew to keep him satisfied and keep him there. She had worked hard for this chance at security. She was sick of working and supporting herself and now that Christian's status as an artist was increasing she could see herself as a prominent member of this new social milieu. She knew he was especially vulnerable now and his guilt about sleeping with her would work to her advantage. Now was the time to tell him that she had let the lease on her flat go. He did not need to know however that she had made this decision a month ago.

Madeline and Michael were out so the only one to witness her performance was Max and she was aware that he disapproved of her anyway. She believed his soulful canine eyes expressed constant criticism and when Christian was out she kept him locked in the coat room. No dog was going to make her feel guilty. She sidled up to Christian who was sitting nursing a mug of cold tea and slid her arm around him and kissed him on the cheek.

"Last night was very special Chris. It meant so much to me that you have forgiven me for they way I treated you in the past. You are such a decent man."

And she meant to take advantage of that decency. She hoped the tears that she was forcing into her eyes looked convincing.

"Seeing our son and his wonderful future bride bathed so radiantly in one another's love made me realise that I never really gave enough to our marriage or to you. I want to make it up to you. And judging by your response last night I know you still feel something for me. I know I stuffed up before Chris but I have changed. I did not appreciate what I had before and I honestly believe we could make it work this time."

She decided to ignore the look of dread and confusion that was washing over his handsome face.

"Rhonda it is not quite as simple as that." He countered. He looked at the tears luminescent in her eyes and remembered her naked body in his bed last night and was unable to continue. He did not want her in his life or bed again but could not tell her so at this moment.

"Don't you have a job and a flat waiting for you in London?" He asked hopefully.

"Actually I resigned and my flat has been sold. The landlord rang me during the week. I have to be out in three weeks. I thought I might look for something in this area. I assume that I can continue to stay here until I find something? You can give me that at least can't you?"

He thought of Julia and the gallery opening and the way he had treated her and he was paralysed with indecision. There was no right response. No matter what he said someone would be hurt. Rhonda saw the indecision flash across his face and wanted to forestall a negative response so launched her backup plan.

"I will have to head up to London next weekend anyway to organise the storage of my furniture. I may be gone for a week. You can manage without me for that time I am sure. I'm afraid I will miss your opening though." She said with feigned regret.

The window of opportunity this presented to Christian was the reprieve he needed.

"Of course you can stay until you find something Rhonda but you should really think carefully about moving back here. You found it provincial and boring once and it hasn't changed."

"But I have darling." She reassured.

Christian did not for one moment believe this to be true and when a vision of the past flashed before her neither did Rhonda.

With Rhonda gone for a week or so Christian hoped he could smooth things over with Julia. He could still collect her from the airport and she could attend the opening. The more time he was forced to spend with Rhonda the more he missed Julia. He had tried to tell her how he really felt but each time he attempted to broach the subject she diverted him and after a lifetime of giving in to her demands inertia set in and he found himself paralysed. Day after day he rehearsed a forceful yet tactful way of saying that they had no future together but it was all dress- rehearsal and no performance.

He needed to see Julia, he needed to touch her warm skin and look into those eyes that always reflected what she felt. She was incapable of wearing a mask and he knew exactly how her eyes would have looked when he so unfairly attacked her. He cringed again at the unbidden image. He had hoped she would ring him but knew she would be uncertain of her reception. It was up to him to try and make it right, he would ring her after breakfast and grovel if need be. He clung to the hope that Julia knew he had not meant what he said. She must realise that it was just a jealous and immature reaction to the photo. He would finally tell Rhonda they had no future together but first he had to speak to Julia. He would ring from the studio as it was the only place that afforded him any privacy. He walked to the kitchen to grab his phone from its usual spot but could not find it.

"Rhonda, have you seen my phone?"

"No darling."

It grated each time she used this insincere endearment and he found that his fists were clenched.

"I'm sure I left it on the bench. Are you sure you didn't move it?"

"I have no interest in your mobile Chris. Perhaps you left it in the studio?"

"Okay, I'll look there. Have a safe trip to London and enjoy the bustle and stimulation, you certainly won't get that if you move back here."

Christian walked out to his studio praying fervently that Rhonda would stay put in London. He horrified himself with a momentary unbidden wish that she meet with misadventure on the way.

He searched the studio thoroughly but was unable to locate his er-

rant mobile. He started the short drive to the gallery with a slowly mounting excitement. The opening was only days away and hopefully after an abject and heartfelt apology Julia would forgive him and return as she had promised. He would ring from the gallery phone and say and do whatever was necessary to ensure that he would see her again. There was an autumn chill in the air but the sky was blue and the sun shining and his spirits lifted and he started to whistle. He felt that with her by his side he would have the strength to be honest with Rhonda but first he just needed to hear her voice.

He unlocked the gallery door and looked around with a sense of pride. It was like walking into an underwater cave. The white walls embraced the paintings with passion and care. The block-mounted canvasses that had been stacked on the floor were now hung asymmetrically on one wall. The vista of blues and greens and the myriad textural finishes swamped the senses. He felt like he was a child walking barefoot through soft green grass. The warm sand lay ahead and the cooling ocean offered instant respite from the heat. His doubts about the future suddenly vanished. He knew where he was headed and who he wanted by his side and his desire to share this moment with Julia was intense.

He almost tripped over his own feet in his eagerness to reach the phone. H e lifted the handset and went to dial and realised with a start that he had no idea of Julia's mobile number, he knew no phone numbers in fact. Everybody he knew was just a number on speed dial or a name in his phone's address book. Without his phone he was like a marooned Robinson Caruso. The feeling of disappointment was so crushing he started to hyperventilate. He closed his eyes and slowed his breathing and remembered that she was staying at the Hilton hotel. He would call her there and if she wasn't in her room at least he could leave a message. She would know that he was sorry and missed her at least.

He picked up the handset again called directory assistance and then the hotel and a cheerful transatlantic voice asked how she might be of service.

"I would like to speak to a guest please. Her name is Julia Kennedy. I don't know the room number." He asked with a feeling of increasing hope and excitement.

"Hold the line a moment sir and I will check. I'm sorry we have no

one currently registered under that name."

He was certain that was where she was staying.

"I'm sorry but could you please check again. I know she was staying there."

He could hear the clatter of computer keys and he tried to keep under control his rising panic.

"We did have a guest under that name sir, but she checked out early this morning."

"Did she by any chance leave a forwarding address?" He asked with little hope of a positive response.

"I'm sorry sir, she didn't. Can I assist you in any other way?"

He hung up as the elation and certainty he had felt only moments before rushed from his body like a tidal wave. He had to find his mobile and he would empty out his whole house if need be. He berated himself again for his behaviour as he tried to imagine where Julia might be. If he couldn't contact her he would just have to meet her flight in the hope that she would be true to her word. Not that he deserved her he thought dismally.

Rhonda had a secret. Rhonda in fact had many secrets but there was one that was so new and exciting she hugged herself when she thought of it. Madeline had an uncle, a very handsome uncle with a sexy French accent and a cultivated appreciation of women. Claude attended the engagement party and when Rhonda was not draped on her ex-husband's arm he showered her with lavish compliments. His unabashed appreciation of her trim figure and his flirtatious behaviour did not go unnoticed by Rhonda or indeed by Madeline. She had smiled to herself during the evening and had even said to Michael,

"Look, uncle Claude is on the make again. I think he might meet his match in your mother though."

Rhonda's obvious interest made Madeline's shock even greater when she saw Christian slinking out of Rhonda's room the next morning. She thought she was quite worldly and sophisticated but when she saw the mistakes and infidelities of the older generation she felt young and inexperienced. She also felt very sorry for Julia who although she tried to hide behind humour and a casual attitude radiated passion. She knew that Julia was in love with Christian even if she did not acknowledge it herself and Christian must be blind if he couldn't see it. Julia had had a lot of hurt in her life and she hated the thought of her suffering more at Christian's cavalier hands.

Rhonda however was not suffering, she was soaring. Claude had been sending her flirty text messages for weeks and she was meeting him for dinner in London tonight. She had high hopes for this affair, the sexy French lover and hopefully the decent man in England to support her as well. She was always happiest when she had two men in her life. If she was discreet Chris would not find out. Still, it's early days yet, she thought Claude may not live up to expectations. But now she needed to max out the credit card on a dress seductive enough to make him salivate. They were dining at the Ritz and she assumed he was staying overnight there. The suites were supposed to be amazing and she wondered if she would get to see it later. A delicious thrill of anticipation coursed through her body. Money spent on this dress could really be viewed as an investment, she thought.

23

I WAITED DAY AFTER DAY hoping that Christian would ring. I kept my mobile by my side and obsessively checked my room phone for messages. Eventually I decided that righteous indignation was souring my days so I gave in and rang his mobile only to hear that same sad message—"this phone is turned off or out of mobile range." I couldn't believe that he was being this petty. "Stuff him!" I thought. I have spent enough days and nights agonising over that horrible phone call. It was time to get on with enjoying my trip and the company of my children.

Josh wanted to go on a road trip to Salem. Witches and the Salem witch trials had long fascinated him and all the Halloween decorations had reawakened his interest. He tried hard to be cool and laid back but his natural enthusiasm and quirky outlook kept bubbling through. He made the prospect sound so enticing that he soon had us both convinced.

I checked out of the hotel, picked up a hire car and the three of us set off for Boston with great enthusiasm. As they were both under twenty-five and deemed too great an insurance risk I was the designated driver. This did not stop them from driving from the back seat however and after myriad conflicting instructions, screams and laughter we finally left the city and hit the open road.

Autumn in New England is stunning—the richness of the claret reds, the burnt oranges and the golden yellows of the changing foliage entranced us all. We stopped a number of times just so they could run through the fallen leaves as they had as children. They crunched the dried leaves underfoot and tried to bury one another under the leafy piles. There were still pumpkins adorning the doorsteps of the timber-clad houses and a cornucopia of fresh produce at market stalls. Time seemed to have reversed and I was transported back ten years to a school holiday jaunt in the Southern Highlands of New South Wales. I fully expected them to start complaining about school uniforms and uncompleted assignments. We arrived in Boston tired, happy and enriched by the sensuality of our day.

We were just ordering an after dinner coffee when Josh leapt from the table and excused himself to take a call. He removed the vibrating phone from his pocket and walked towards the bar while I had flashbacks to my own tipsy encounter with a vibrating phone. It felt like a lifetime ago but still had the power to make me cringe.

Christian was firmly in my mind again and I wondered what he was doing right now. Was he at the gallery? Had everything been completed? I still could not believe how angry he had been. The accusations he had hurled at me still chilled. I was choosing to believe that he had lashed out because he was hurt and jealous. But if I was honest with myself I had to admit that I did not really know him. If I could just see his face I was sure I could see the truth. Had I delude myself about what we felt? It had felt so right when we were together but time and distance were making me doubt not only what he felt but also what I felt. I did not know whether the rift could be repaired.

When Josh reached the bar he hoisted himself onto a bar stool and with studied nonchalance leant one elbow on the countertop and wrapped one leg around the stool. He turned to face us and smiled self-consciously. Rebecca nudged me and said half with pride and half with amusement, "Behold, the rock-star at leisure!" His face suddenly paled and his eyes widened then a smile that seemed to start at his toes washed over his face. His head was nodding and he was uttering 'yes' repeatedly and trying to contain an eruption of excitement. His cool demeanour evaporated as he raced back to us, pulled us to our feet and danced us around the table. His joy was infectious and other diners forsaking their customary New England reserve looked across and smiled.

"Josh what on earth has happened?" We both said in unison.

"That was our manager on the phone. Another band has suddenly pulled out of a music festival and they want us to fill in. We get a twenty minute spot. They want us to perform our new single. It's such an amazing line-up, I can't believe it."

"What festival?" Rebecca asked.

"I can't remember. *Live* something or other, you know the sort of thing, save the whales, save the planet, save the hungry. Whatever it is I'm sure I can become a fervent supporter by Saturday. I can tell already that whatever the issue is I have been supporting it since childhood." He said with a wry grin.

"I'm so happy for you and so proud." I said squeezing his hand and drinking at the fountain of maternal pride.

"I'll have to fly back in the morning though. No more road trip for this soon to be famous musician." He joked. "Seriously though, can you come?" He said as his eyes encompassed us both. "I will have backstage passes."

"Try to keep me away brother. Think of all the real musicians I can meet." Rebecca said grinning at him. "When is it?"

"This Sunday. Please tell me you can come too mum." His eagerness was heart melting.

"Josh I don't think it is very cool to have your mother backstage."

"Mum, I don't care about cool. I want the people I love to share it with me. Anyway you always commented on how lovely Robbie Williams must be because he often has his mum backstage." He said pointedly.

I was about to say 'yes' but pulled myself up when I realised that Christian's gallery opening was the coming weekend too. I didn't know what to do. I wanted to be there for Josh and was touched beyond words that he wanted me there but I had promised Christian too. I had no idea if he even still wanted me there. I had to talk to him before I could commit to Josh. Steve and I had always taught Rebecca and Josh to live up to their promises even from a young age. If they had accepted an invitation they kept it even if a better one came in later. I had to at least try to do the same.

We left the restaurant and walked back to the hotel in the chill of the evening.

"Josh, I'm not sure if I can go. I have somewhere else I promised to be this weekend."

They both looked at me with questioning faces and Josh tried hard to mask his disappointment. I would have to explain. I should have done it weeks ago and the whole sorry fight with Christian may never have occurred.

"I have been seeing someone ... in England ... an old friend from when I was younger." They looked at me encouragingly so I garnered the courage to continue.

"His name is Christian and he is an artist and I have been helping him with his gallery which opens this weekend."

"I think that's great mum," Rebecca said as she wrapped her arm around my waist. "Why didn't you tell us?"

"I thought you would think that I hadn't loved your father." I said sheepishly.

They looked at one another and shook their heads.

"Sometimes parents can be really dense can't they Josh? You must go then mum if you promised. You drilled it into our heads often enough. Josh will have plenty of other concerts when he is rich and famous, won't you?" She said turning to her brother with a pointed look.

"Yes, of course mum. I understand." But his face did not mirror what his voice was saying ... "When do we meet him?"

"Well things are sort of complicated. We had a fight and I haven't been able to contact him and I'm not certain the opening is still on schedule. So I may get to L.A. yet." I spared them the gruesome details of the fight but Rebecca was not to be deterred.

"How could you fight if you are on opposite sided of the Atlantic?" She queried.

"Remember that call you took on my mobile the night of the Halloween ball..."

"That was him ... Oh shit! I told him you were on a date didn't I? But didn't you explain?"

"I did but he also saw that photo you accidentally emailed to Madeline. She is his son's fiancée." A look of intense mortification flooded her face. "It's not your fault Bec. It was just one of those stupid misunderstandings that escalated. I'm sure it will all blow over as soon as I can speak to him but his mobile is off and the gallery number is not listed yet."

"Mum, I am so sorry and to think I set you up with Professor Stevens. You should have said something. He must think I am an idiot ... He was quite impressed by you, you know."

"He is a very nice man and don't worry, I told him all about Christian before I agreed to go to the ball."

We walked along a little further in silence and Rebecca seemed to be lost in thought. I hoped she wasn't blaming herself for the mix up or reading more into my relationship with Christian than there really was. In all likelihood it would probably turn out to be just a fling that I would get over in time. I had sought a no strings affair and maybe that's all it actually was. We had reached the entrance to the hotel when she turned to me and said,

"I've got an idea mum. Why don't you email Madeline. She must have a number for your man or at least know about the gallery dates."

I kissed her on the forehead and said, "Why didn't I think of that. Your young brain works well when it is not impaired by tequila." She had the grace to look sheepish.

They both fell asleep the second their heads hit their pillows just as they had as children while I logged onto my laptop and tried to compose an email to Madeline. What do I say? Why is Christian refusing to take my calls? Did he really mean the things he said? Is Rhonda still there and does he still want me there for the opening? I wanted to go to Josh's concert but not if it jeopardised a reconciliation with Christian. It felt very alien to contemplate putting the needs of another man before that of my child.

I decided to be as honest and straightforward as I could without revealing too much. Not an easy task. I did not really know what I was feeling. We had made no promises about a future and I found it hard at this stage to envisage one. I did not understand why he had not received my messages and texts. Perhaps he was lying about that to justify his own behaviour. It had seemed so much clearer when he held me and the outside world was not hammering at my door. What had he said to me at the airport? Increments, one step at a time. Well, I guess the next step must be to find out if he genuinely wanted me to return for his big night.

> Dear Madeline,
>
> Josh is playing at a concert in L.A. this weekend and has asked me to attend. I had told Christian that I would be back for the opening but have been unable to contact him to confirm our arrangements. I have called repeatedly but he is not taking my calls. I know Bec has explained and apologised to you for the photo debacle. Is he still upset about it?
>
> I would be happiest if he rang me in person but I will be guided by you. I trust your judgement. I think you have a wise head on those young shoulders. I need to change flights if I am going to LA so if you could give me an indication of how Christian is feeling I would be very grateful. Your wedding jewellery is well underway and looking stunning by the way.
>
> Merci beacoup, a bientot,
>
> Julia.

The kids were both up early and I put off checking my email as long as I could. I needed to get Josh to the airport by lunchtime so could delay no longer. My heart skipped a beat when I saw a reply from Madeline in my inbox. I opened the message and read it twice.

"Come on Josh, hurry up or you will miss your flight. I would hate to see you up on stage without adequate rehearsal." I said as I grabbed the car keys and pushed him out the door.

"Does that mean you can come?" He asked trying to disguise the lilt of hope in his voice.

"It certainly does. I will be the oldest groupie backstage and loving every minute of it."

Rebecca looked up from the book she was reading with a question in her eyes. I gave her my brightest smile but I don't think she was convinced.

He walked onto the stage with a practised swagger, flung his guitar across his shoulder and took his place behind the microphone. He chewed on his bottom lip nervously while his band-mates took their places. He shook his hair as if dispelling it of nerves and shouted out, "G'day L.A. we are *The Cards* and this is our new single."

I held my breath waiting for them to start. It felt like being at the 2000 Sydney Olympics when the whole of Australia held its breath in a mixture of fear and pride as they waited for Cathie Freeman to light the Olympic torch. The brief technical glitch had seemed like hours and we collectively feared global embarrassment but like now it proved unfounded. The guitar riff started slow and built to a crescendo of rock glory as Josh's voice rang out. They sounded amazing and as I turned and faced Bec her face mirrored mine, eyes shining and tears glistening her cheeks. The crowd erupted onto its feet and applause and cheers echoed through the stadium. I was proud and happy that I could be here for the start of what was obviously going to be a stellar career. I had seen Josh and the band perform many times before in Sydney but that had been merely the pregnancy leading up to this spectacular birth. He turned his head towards the wings and caught my gaze, smiled and mouthed 'thankyou'. I was certain that I had made the right decision. So why did I feel so empty?

It seemed that whenever I turned on the radio over the next two weeks *The Cards* were playing. Their single had debuted at 100 but was rapidly making its way up the charts and there was a buzz about their performance and their future. I walked into record stores just so I could watch people buying their CD. I resisted the urge to rush up to strangers and say 'that's my son you know.' Josh was busy with performances and promotion and I had seen little of him in the past week. Rebecca had reluctantly returned to college. She was excited about her own career but loath to leave the exhilaration of the rock scene. I took her to the airport and as we waited for her flight to be called she summoned up courage and asked,

"What happened with Christian mum, you haven't so much as mentioned his name since Boston?"

"It just wasn't meant to be I guess." I offered. As the words left my mouth I knew it was an inadequate explanation.

"Did Madeline answer your email?" She was obviously going to persist until she had a satisfactory answer. But what was adequate? Do I tell her how he made me feel and how my heart felt if not broken at least severely bruised. I saw the concern and the intelligence in her blue eyes and realised although she was my child she was an adult. She deserved the truth.

"Madeline told me, reluctantly I imagine, that she saw him leaving his ex-wife's bedroom early the morning after the engagement party. He did not see her apparently. It would appear that they are back together again and she has moved in. Madeline's loyalty was severely tested. She did not want to betray her prospective father-in-law but she did not want to see me hurt or made a fool of either."

"Poor Madeline ... poor you." She said as she wrapped her arms around me.

It was an unaccustomed sensation to be comforted by my own child but I rested my head on her shoulder and drew succour from her embrace.

"Will you be okay mum?" She asked.

"I will. This is merely a hiccough after all we have been through. Don't mention anything to Madeline if you speak to her though. I asked her not to tell Michael or his dad that she had told me. You know the thing that really hurts Bec, is that he did not have the decency to tell me himself. I think he owed me that much. I guess I did not know him as well as I thought I did."

"I'll tell you what you always tell me mum. If he can't see what an amazing person you are then he is not worth having in your life. You'll meet someone again who truly deserves you, someone who is not a lying cheater." The use of this childish term made me smile and reminded me that she really was not that far from childhood

"I love you." She said as she picked up her backpack and made her way to the gate.

"I love you too."

I watched her disappear from sight. I was very sick of saying goodbye to those I loved.

I spent a week catching up with some old neighbours who had moved to Santa Barbara about ten years ago. We laughed over old times and some of our legendary parties. John had been close to Steve, more friends than neighbours and he had been upset that he had been too far away to spend much time with him in those last months. While sipping chardonnay and barbecuing steaks on their back patio his presence felt very strong.

Jess had emailed me to tell me that Zoe and her husband had bought a house and would be moving out of mine in two weeks. I was starting to feel very homesick and longed to see the Pacific Ocean under an Australian summer sun. The overcast wintery skies here cast a grey tinge to the ocean and instead of providing its usual invigorating appeal it was having the polar effect and depressing me. The solution was simple; head home and enjoy a Sydney summer in my own home. The allure of living out of a suitcase, or many suitcases as it was by now, had paled. So I booked a flight home and within the week I was ensconced in the Qantas lounge at LAX sipping an Australian champagne and trying to find the meaning and upside of my adventures.

I had set out in the hope of reconnecting with my real self, the younger me that had not been weighed down by disappointment and loss. I had wanted to feel again and be desired again. I had wanted to have sex, uncomplicated glorious sex with a good looking man. I had not set out looking for ties and commitment. I had achieved all this and more. I felt younger, more attractive, more desirable than when I had left home. I was confident that Rebecca and Josh were both making their own way in the world quite happily and a wave of contentment washed over me. My life really was not so bad. My anger at Christian had left me and I realised with startling clarity that I had expected too much from him; expected him to meet my unstated and unacknowledged demands.

He had given me what I needed—acknowledgement that I was

still attractive and still sexual and I was grateful for that but it was now time to move on. Time to move on and without regrets.

I was startled out of my reverie by the shrill cry of my mobile. I assumed it would be Rebecca or Josh wishing me bon voyage and quickly checked the caller I.D. before flipping it open. But the name that flashed so insistently at me was *Christian.* Not now, he could not do this to me now. I considered for a moment not answering but my curiosity won out. What possible explanation could he offer at this stage?

"Hello, Julia Kennedy speaking."

24

CHRISTIAN WAS TORN between excitement about the gallery opening and worry about Julia. The guest list had grown exponentially in the last week; it seemed that everyone wanted an invite. He had to put in an urgent request to Merilyn to increase the catering numbers and she in turn had to organise extra wait staff. Fortunately there were always students looking to pick up extra work so that problem had been easily solved.

Rhonda thankfully had extended her stay in London so he had shelved that problem in the short term. He had finally decided to be frank with her and explain that there was no future relationship for them outside of what already existed. He would explain that they had given it their best shot many times but it was never enough. They would always have Michael in common and possibly future grandchildren he thought with alarm. He knew that he could never love her and he did not believe that she suddenly loved him. He did not understand how she was able to manipulate him so easily but even when he agreed to her requests he suspected he was being duped. He could not however prevent her from com-

ing to live near him or throw her trademark tantrums. He had already said she could stay till she found somewhere to live and he felt obliged to honour that commitment. God give him the strength to deal with it all he prayed.

He still had no way of contacting Julia and no idea of where she might be but in his mind because he had theoretically disposed of Rhonda he assumed that Julia would be ready to re-enter his life. This time she would be invited and welcomed with open arms. He longed to hold her again and he fervently believed that all obstacles would melt away the minute she melted into his embrace.

He would explain about his lapse with Rhonda and beg her forgiveness for his stupidity and jealousy. There had been a link between them for over twenty years and he felt sure it could sustain a little more pressure. He was relieved none the less that she knew nothing of his lapse with Rhonda. He would tell her when the time seemed right. He suspected that if she knew now she would not believe that he had truly ostracized Rhonda from his heart and head. He knew logically that it was unreasonable to expect her to return for the opening after the way he had treated her but she had promised that she would come back and he clung to the belief.

Her plane was due at 2p.m. and he was at the airport in plenty of time. He felt foolish standing there with a bouquet of flowers but he thought the image, cut straight from a Hollywood film would amuse her. The airline had refused to give him information about their passenger list even when he flashed his dimple beguilingly at the middle-aged reservation clerk.

He had imagined the scene so often in his head he could have scripted it. She would walk through the barrier wheeling her luggage scanning the crowd for sight of him. She would smile tentatively at first but when she saw his answering smile and the flowers she would laugh and hurry her pace towards him. There would be a moment of awkwardness while he apologised. He would look into her eyes and see that he was forgiven and then he would kiss her and she would respond unmindful of those around them. It felt so real his lips tingled with her touch.

He had been unable to find his mobile and had finally bought a new one and was gradually adding numbers to it as friends and artists contacted him. The one number he wanted however was the one he did not have. But such was his faith in his vision and her steadfastness that he was not concerned when passenger after passenger disembarked and Julia was not among them. His heart started racing when the last group of passengers came through the arrivals gate. There was a brunette woman in their midst and he started to walk towards her when two young children raced up and wrapped their eager arms around her legs. Her resemblance to Julia was superficial but so great was his belief in the likelihood of her appearance that it took him some seconds to process the differences.

He stood there so forlornly that the reservation clerk who had denied his request earlier took pity on him and checked the incoming passenger lists for the remainder of the day. No Julia Kennedy was listed on any flight that day. His disappointment was palpable and the clerk felt sorry for him and herself. No man especially one as attractive as Christian had ever longed for her company to that extent. Her shift was finished and she walked out of the terminal building with him. In a vain attempt to offer him hope she said,

"Perhaps she got the day wrong."

"Perhaps she did. Thankyou, for your help. Would I be breaking any aviation regulations if I gave you these?" He said proffering her the dozen red roses.

She accepted them happily and inhaled their heady scent wondering yet again how any woman could stand him up. She watched him walk to his car with a heaviness to his tread. He raised his hand to brush his hair from his forehead and he turned and waved. She moved the bouquet to her other arm and waved in return and she moved to her own car with more of a bounce to her step than usual.

There were so many people crammed into the gallery that the students taking around the food platters had to breathe in and turn sideways to get through. The noise level rose as more and more wine was consumed. Chequebooks were out in force and almost every painting wore a red sticker with pride. The local press were there taking photos and copy and Christian was sure he had been photographed more in the last hour than over the last ten years. The food had been fulsomely praised and

Merilyn had been offered more catering jobs than she could deal with. She was seriously considering expanding her business and taking on full-time staff.

A buyer from London had asked one of the young artists to see more of Christian's work. The only canvas that was not already hung was of a moonlit beach. It was so evocative that you could hear the breeze rustling the palm fronds and feel the humidity in the air. There was a giant turtle laying eggs in the white sand. Its ancient back reflected the moonlight and its eyes showed the wisdom of age. There were two figures in the painting, a young man and a woman whose long dark hair was uplifted by the breeze. They stood side by side silhouetted in the moonlight. There was a great stillness and serenity to the painting. The buyer looked down to see the title ***"Inception"*** *and decided that he must have it.*

He sought Christian out and introduced himself.

"Congratulations on a splendid turn out. You obviously have some talented young artists under your wing but your work is in a class of its own. I'm surprised I haven't heard of you before."

"Thankyou for the kind words. Yes, I believe a number of the students will make a name for themselves in the art world. That is one of the reasons I have started the gallery to give a canvas for their canvasses, so to speak." It was about the tenth time he had made the lame pun that evening and he grimaced as he uttered it.

"I have made a couple of purchases but there is a larger work of yours I would like to buy but it is not listed in the catalogue."

"That's strange. Point it out to me."

"It's resting against a wall in the back storeroom. "Inception" I think it was called."

Christian's face paled but he recovered quickly and said,

"I'm sorry but it is not for sale ... I painted it as a gift for someone who was unable to be here tonight. However I do have other canvasses in my studio at home. If you leave me your details I will arrange for you to view them at your convenience."

The buyer swallowed his disappointment and agreed to see Christian's other work but as a parting entreaty he offered,

"I would offer you a very generous price if you change your mind."

"I will keep it in mind but I still hope to give it to the person I painted

it for."

One of the local journalists was in earshot of this exchange and directed her photographer to take a quick snap of the painting in question.

"There could be a very interesting human interest story behind this painting," she said to her photographer, "a good looking artist, the mystery woman and the painting he refuses to sell. My female readers will lap this up. Sex, romance and mystery—a perfect combination."

She blended into the crowd notebook in hand to garner as much information as she could about the painting and its artist and the mystery prospective recipient.

The crowd started to thin and the queue of customers completing their purchases dwindled. Christian poured himself a glass of wine, his first for the evening and he looked up with hope as he had all evening as he heard the bell on the door ring. It was Merilyn returning from taking another load out to her van. She looked exhausted but happy. She kicked of her black heels and sat heavily on the leather bench. He poured her a glass of wine, kissed her on the cheek and thanked her for all her hard work.

"It was a brilliant evening Chris. People will be talking about it for weeks. I thought Julia might have made it back. She would be very proud of how well it went especially after all her input." She looked at him quizzically hoping for an explanation.

"I hoped she'd be here too." He replied avoiding her gaze.

"Dare I ask what went wrong?"

Christian shrugged but said nothing. Merilyn sipped her wine and the last of the guests departed. She got up and locked the door and hobbled back in her stockinged feet to Christian.

"I know it is not my place and you will probably tell me to butt out but I feel I have known you long enough to offer unsolicited advice."

Christian looked at her with a look of resignation so she continued.

"I don't know what happened with you and Julia but I can guarantee it involved Rhonda. Everything that has ever gone wrong in your life has involved Rhonda. Please don't let her creep back in and poison everything again. Life's too short Chris to relive old mistakes."

"You are right as usual and I really am severing ties with Rhonda

this time. I foolishly thought Julia would turn up even though I had treated her badly. Maybe she is not the person I thought she was."

"Maybe she is Chris ... perhaps you just need to sort out your life first. You can't have a relationship with any woman while Rhonda still pulls the strings. Now I am going to shut up and go home." She walked over and hugged him tight. "Goodnight."

He locked the door behind her and walked through the empty gallery. In every corner he could see signs of Julia's touch. His need to share his triumph with her produced a physical ache. He removed one of the sold works from the wall and replaced it with Julia's canvass. He stared at it intently and relived the moment it depicted until he felt her near him in time if not space. "Where are you Julia? Why aren't you here?" To his embarrassment his eyes welled with tears and he wiped them angrily away.

The photographer was returning to his car when he chanced upon this well-lit tableau. He knew he should not intrude upon this private moment but he was experienced at overriding his better feelings so he furtively clicked off another few frames.

Christian was extremely busy over the next two weeks and true to his word the London buyer had been out to his studio and paid more than generously for two canvasses with promises to direct more business his way. Rhonda thankfully was still tied up in London or so she said, so he had been unable to have the showdown he had rehearsed so frequently. Still, the longer she was away the easier it would be. She had rung earlier today asking if she had left her passport there. When he queried her need for her passport she fobbed him off with some feeble explanation about needing extra I.D. for the bank. She still called him darling and it still grated.

He entered Rhonda's bedroom reluctantly. Her cloying scent polluted the air and the unbidden image of their tryst polluted his mind. He rifled through her underwear drawer and found the passport but when he went to close it the drawer stuck. He reached to the back and found a pair of socks had caught on the back of the drawer. They were strangely heavy so he pulled them out to have a better look. It was obvious there was something hidden inside and with curiosity he unrolled the socks. A mobile phone fell out, his mobile phone, the phone that Rhonda swore she had no knowledge of. He was so angry that if she had been present he would have throttled her. Instead he took out his anger on her belongings.

Everything she had left behind he threw into cardboard boxes, clothes, shoes, cosmetics, perfumes. He did not replace lids on make-up bottles and if he had thought of the damage leaking perfume would inflict on silk clothing he would have been pleased.

He vacuumed the room and used bleach and highly scented lemon furniture polish on every surface till all scent of her was gone. He contemplated destroying her passport but feared it was a government offence and he was reluctant to destroy any means by which she might leave the country and his life. The boxes he placed outside the front door so she would not have an excuse to put so much as a toe across his threshold again.

Only when all this was completed did he think about the phone itself. He poured himself a large scotch even though it was barely 11 a.m. and plugged the phone into the charger. The battery was completely dead so it took a while for there to be enough charge to turn it on again. He spent that time drinking another scotch and sharing with Max the iniquities of his ex-wife. When the battery indicator showed that there was sufficient charge he put the phone on loudspeaker and listened to almost four weeks of messages. It was strange. No messages received showed on his inbox but when he rang voicemail there were dozens. Rhonda must have deleted the text messages. His anger rose again and he downed his drink in one.

The first voice he heard was Julia's and Max pricked up his ears and his tail beat out an excited rhythm on the floor.

"Hi Christian, arrived safely in New York. Sorry I did not ring last night but was exhausted. I miss you already. Ring me."

"I still keep missing you. My bed is very lonely. Wish you were here with me. I guess the opening is keeping you very busy. Please ring me."

"I'm going to a Halloween ball tonight. I'll tell you all about it later if we ever manage to connect. I've got some great ideas for a private costume party."

"Christian I miss you. I can't believe you thought any of those hurtful things you said. It has taken me days to get up the courage to ring you. Please talk to me. I know we can work this out."

"Messagebank again! I can think of no reason why you are refusing to talk to me other than the obvious. If you don't want to see me again have the courtesy to tell me."

This message brought Christian undone as Julia sobbed at the end of it.

"This is the last message I am going to leave. In case it still matters to you I have told Bec and Josh all about you finally and yes, I should have done it sooner. I want to return for the opening as I promised. Do you still want me there? If I don't hear from you I will email Madeline, perhaps she knows what's going on."

"Okay, so it wasn't the last message. At least I now know what is going on. I hope you and Rhonda can make it work this time. I feel like a fool Christian but you made no promises so I can't complain. Good luck with the gallery. I am confident it will be a wonderful success. You are so much more talented than you realise. Don't sell yourself short. I am not sorry we reconnected but some things should obviously be left in the past. The only thing I regret is that the last time I heard your voice it was in anger. Your voicemail message may be chirpy but it is no substitute for the real thing. Goodbye Christian."

Christian sat stunned and he was oblivious to the tears that coursed down his face. Max's excitement at hearing Julia's voice was replaced by confusion and what looked like an accusing stare. He reached his hand out to console the dog and said repeatedly,

"I'm sorry Max. I didn't know. I didn't mean for any of this to happen. Perhaps it's not too late."

He cringed when he thought of the way Julia had found out about Rhonda. It sounded as though she knew that they had slept together but how? The thought that Madeline must have seen him made him cringe anew. Welcome to the family Madeline, a crazy manipulative mother-in-law and a self centred, naïve cheating father-in-law. He did not think it was possible to feel this low. Lower than a dog, he thought. Sorry Max, present company excepted.

"Will she even speak to me if I ring her now Max? I think I need to clear my head, how about a walk."

Max lumbered to his feet with less ease than usual and Christian realised how old the dog was getting.

The walk did little to assuage Christian's guilt but it did strengthen his resolve. He would ring Julia and try to explain. If he had thought to get Julia's email or mobile number from Madeline the debacle could have been avoided. Or perhaps not, he thought, the real deal breaker may still be that he had slept with Rhonda. He would ring when they got back to the house. Any effects of the alcohol had long since departed and he was not going to procrastinate any longer. He dialled her number which he had now committed to memory and listened to each long ring tone. With each unanswered ring he willed her to pick up but was none the less surprised when she finally answered.

"Hello, Julia Kennedy speaking."

"Julia it's Christian."

A long silence greeted him before she said,

"Yes, I know."

"Where are you?" He kicked himself for asking the standard inane mobile phone question but he hoped to hear her say that she was nearby.

"I am at LA airport waiting for my flight to be called."

"Are you on your way back here?" The hope in his voice was palpable and she hesitated before she dashed that hope.

"No, I am going home ... I've been away long enough ... How did the gallery opening go?"

"It was great, big crowd, lots of positive press coverage."

"I'm really pleased Christian."

"I waited for you at the airport Julia."

"What, you and Rhoda both?"

"Just me Julia. Rhonda is no longer an issue."

"I think I heard that before and it wasn't quite true."

"But this time it is .The conniving bitch hid my phone. I never got any of your messages and I didn't know your number. I rang the hotel but you had already checked out ... Do you believe me?"

"I believe you Christian. It explains a lot but it doesn't change anything. It doesn't excuse the fact that you didn't trust me and it doesn't excuse the fact that you so easily fell under her spell again. I'm sorry but it is all just too hard."

"It doesn't have to be hard." He pleaded.

"Perhaps it shouldn't be but it is. I know that I am at fault too. I expected too much of you even though I never told you what I expected. I am used to coming first in the life of a man I love. I'm not prepared to be pushed aside when my presence proves inconvenient."

All Christian heard of this was the word love and he latched onto to it like a life raft.

"Does that mean that you love me?"

"That's not what I meant. Steve and I always put one another first and that is what love is about. I don't think you are ready for love in your life anyway—even if the ex is not in your bed she is still in your head—always there with a pointy- toed shoe ready to kick out anyone who could make you happy."

Christian knew that this time he had exorcised Rhonda for good and the seconds ticked over as he tried to think of an argument that would convince Julia but failed.

"Are you still there Christian?"

"Yes. I'm still here."

"The time we spent together was wonderful. You made me feel desired and happy and I thank you for that but there is no future for us."

He could hear the Qantas flight to Sydney being called over the PA system in the background.

"Julia, you still didn't answer me. Do you love me?"

"Probably Christian, but I will get over it."

"Can I ring you again when you get home?"

"There is not much point is there? It would be painful and pointless to drag it out. Goodbye Christian. I hope you find happiness."

He cradled the phone in his hand long after she had hung up not ready to accept that it could be over so abruptly.

25

I LOOKED OUT THE WINDOW as we began our descent into Sydney. One by one my city's loved landmarks appeared through the clouds and my spirits lifted. It was impossible to feel sad when the sun glinted off the sails of the Opera House and the multicoloured spinnakers of the sail boats darted about the harbour like swarms of butterflies.

But by far the best sight was the megawatt smiles transfiguring the faces of my two closest friends. They raced over to hug me and help me with my heavily laden luggage trolley. There was much kissing and tears and shrieks of laughter as we tried to fit all my bags into Jess's hatchback.

"Is there a shop in L.A or New York that has anything left on the shelves?" Sophie asked as she shoved the last bag onto the back seat. "And didn't you set off unencumbered by check-in luggage? If my memory serves me correct you departed proudly and smugly with a solitary bag."

"You won't complain when you see the things I have bought you."

"You are absolutely forgiven then." They both chorused.

Zoe had stocked my pantry and fridge as a welcome home present and there were even fresh flowers throughout the house. The grass was freshly mown and the pool sparkling. There was fresh linen on all the beds and the house looked more inviting than I had ever seen it yet within three hours of my return and the departure of my good friends I knew that I could no longer live there.

I rang both Rebecca and Josh and asked them if they minded if I sold the house. It had been their home for the last ten years; the home they had shared with their father and I was conscious that I would be severing one more link with the past. After their initial surprise at my sudden decision they both gave me their unqualified support.

"As long as you are there and there is a bed for us any house will be home." Rebecca assured me.

Josh's main concern was his record collection which I promised I would take good care of. They both expressed a long held desire to live near the beach and if the house sold for what the agent predicted I could easily look for an apartment near the sea.

Time seemed to pass at warp speed over the next two months and by the end of January the house was sold and I was busy decorating my new three-bedroom apartment at Bronte in Sydney's east.

The apartment complex was opposite Bronte Park and had views over Nelson Bay. I could walk to the beach and Jess was only fifteen minutes away. I had sent photos to Josh and Rebecca and they had given my choice a hearty tick of approval and were looking forward to putting their unique decorating touch to their bedrooms if they ever returned home. I consoled myself with the fact that I would at least have somewhere to walk a dog – likely my only companion in my imminent old-age.

I was keeping the décor simple with sand coloured walls and scatter rugs on the polished floors. The view of the Pacific Ocean from the living area provided an ever changing background of colour—diamond green, pewter grey and blues from sky blue to cobalt which I mirrored in a selection of scatter cushions on the cream coloured sofas. I was gradually finding paintings and sketches for the walls while trying to stop myself from thinking how wonderful one of Christian's dramatic seascapes would look.

One particular shop was enjoying much of my patronage. It was in a side street but only minutes from both the beach and a dazzling selection of popular cafes and restaurants. It had very erratic opening hours and a great selection of original oils and water-colours from a few local artists interspersed with home-wares and Balinese artefacts. Nothing was displayed to advantage and I was always forced to move canvasses and step over partially unpacked crates to find what I wanted. The window displays swung between quirky and impossibly chaotic. The owner was a charming man in his seventies who flirted with me outrageously.

I had got into the habit of taking him a coffee, a double espresso with two sugars whenever I called in and we would sit and chat about his life and travels. Sophie's birthday was coming up and I was hoping to find a small water-colour for her. Victor drank his coffee, flirted with me as usual and then as I was about to start to rummage for my gift he told me he had some exciting news.

"I am getting married Julia. Her name is Daphne and she has been widowed for ten years. We have decided to throw caution to the winds and go on a round the world cruise for our honeymoon."

I hugged him and offered my congratulations.

"How did you meet?" I asked.

He looked at his feet for a moment, stirred his coffee nervously then said with a look of defiance,

"We met online."

"Then that is even more romantic and exciting. Tell me more. You have actually met haven't you?" I desperately hoped he wasn't being conned into parting with his life savings by an unscrupulous person who preyed on the vulnerable and elderly. His look of exasperation and his reply put me firmly in my place.

"Yes of course! Seventy-four is my age Julia, not my IQ."

I must have looked suitably chastised for he continued.

"She is sixty-eight and very attractive and we have been dating for about six months. She has grown children and grandchildren and is financially secure. At our age love does not come so readily knocking at your door so when it does you grab it."

"Love does not come knocking readily at my age either Victor." I said wistfully.

"Perhaps it knocks and you don't let it in young lady."

Was this the wisdom of age or just the continuation of a bad metaphor?

"I will miss you. What are you doing about the shop while you are away?"

"I wish to sell it but the real estate agent and my accountant don't think it will happen in its present state. What was the polite term they used? I know 'its eclectic demeanour'. I need a buyer who can see its charm already." He looked at me with a question in his eyes.

"Me? But I don't know anything about running a shop."

"It was a gallery first and you seem to know a lot about what makes good art. It could look very different with a young eye and more energy than I have."

I left Victor with a promise to give it some thought and as I walked home a thousand ideas and possibilities swirled through my head. If the junk was cleared out and the back room was used as well there was really quite a lot of wall space. There was plenty of light probably even more if the windows were cleaned. There were already a number of good artists leaving paintings and sketches on consignment and if they were displayed to advantage would sell easily. If it looked more appealing and professional more artists would want to show their work. There must be some ceramic artists who could show as well. It would need a theme to make it stand out. Less windswept but more interesting? I chuckled to myself and felt sad at the same time. It would be a substantial commitment. I still had savings after the sale of the house but I probably would not qualify for a mortgage on the property without a regular income and even if I did manage to buy the business it might not be cash positive for a while.

What I really needed was a partner; someone to share the financial risk; someone I could work with; someone who could see the hidden potential of the business and someone who loved art. Not much to ask at all!

The phone was ringing as I let myself into the apartment but of course stopped just before I could pick up. I had not switched the answer machine on that morning so after I put the cheese, tomatoes and rocket into the fridge I dialled * 10 #. It was Jess's home number which was unusual during the day—perhaps she was home sick from work and needed something.

She did not sound sick when she picked up the phone, in fact she sounded unusually buoyant.

"Julia I am so glad you rang back. I've been made redundant." She stated boldly.

"I'm sorry Jess. What happened?"

"Don't be sorry Julia, it's fantastic. I was bored senseless in my job and I have been given a wickedly huge redundancy package. An American company is taking over and I opted for voluntary redundancy. I am looking forward to a career change. I am over working sixty hours a week and I have plenty of time to find something that I actually might enjoy."

The wheels in my head were spinning at the speed of light.

"Let me take you to lunch Jess and celebrate. No better still come here. I'll whip up that quiche you like so much and put a bottle or two of Moet on ice. There is something I want to show you and I think you will need a drink or two to appreciate its beauty. It might be better if you didn't drive."

The quiche was baking happily in the oven, the rocket, pear and blue cheese salad was made, the baguette was sliced and the champagne was sitting enticingly in the ice bucket. I was just placing the flowers on the table when I saw a taxi pull up and Jess's long legs emerge from the car.

She was dressed casually in white jeans and a burnt-orange singlet and her hair was down. Even her customary high heels were missing and her feet were encased in emerald green ballet flats. She carried a designer bag of the same colour and Dior sunnies were perched on her head. She looked ten years younger out of her corporate attire. She looked up and waved and I buzzed her in.

We ate lunch and sipped our delicious champagne as she told me of the machinations behind the takeover and her redundancy.

"The strange thing is I had already decided to resign before all this happened but now I get to leave with a big payout. Sometimes the gods do smile down on us Julia."

"Talking of gods smiling ... I have a business opportunity that just might interest you."

I outlined all my fledgling ideas concocted in the past two hours and she listened intently, asking pertinent questions most of which I couldn't answer.

"It certainly sounds feasible. Let's go and look at this potential gallery of yours." She said draining the last mouthful of champagne from her glass.

It took her a little longer to see the potential that I saw but she trusted my judgement there. She was brilliant talking with the real estate agent and Victor's accountant and they were able to answer all the questions that I couldn't. She took a sheaf of figures to go over and if the figures stacked up she assured them that we would make an offer. Victor was off on his honeymoon in two weeks and promised us unfettered access to the gallery at any time. As the agent said, he was a 'motivated seller.'

Jess's husband Brad was enthusiastic about the idea and by midday the next day we had made an offer which was accepted. My head was in a whirl and I alternated between euphoria and dread.

Two weeks later we took possession of the premises and some of our initial enthusiasm drained as we faced the daunting task ahead of us. We put what we could into temporary storage and started to clean up. We ripped up the aged carpet and had the floorboards sanded and polished to a pale honey glow. The walls were painted off-white and the timber trims a deep blue. Jess was a brilliant project manager and seemed to know myriad tradespeople who were always available when we wanted them. We had flexible track lighting installed so we could light the art works to advantage; broadband and extra phone lines put in and I had already started designing a website.

Space was at a premium but we needed a small functional kitchen with an espresso machine and fridge—there were some creature comforts we could not do without. The bathroom had barely been used and needed only a coat of paint and small hand basin fitted. It took shape very quickly and passers-by kept calling in and asking what we were doing and they all promised to call back when we opened.

It was my job to discover and negotiate with the artists. Victor's records were as eclectic as his décor but I managed to track down all those who had left paintings and drawings with him. They enthusiastically pledged their support and did not even baulk at the twenty-five percent commission Jess insisted I ask for. I contacted the Sydney art schools and organised to see their shows so I could see what the contemporary scene was offering. Rebecca was ecstatic about the venture and regretted that she was not on hand to help but she provided me with names of painters and sculptors who she stated had talent and should be watched.

We had more than enough works to open with and even a catalogue of artists who wanted to exhibit. We wanted to have revolving exhibitions every few months or four shows a year. On of Rebecca's friends was an art photographer and was taking digital images of all the artists' work for an online catalogue and postcards so even when they weren't exhibiting they still had a showcase for their work. We had decided to open quietly and build momentum gradually but there already seemed to be a snowball effect and first the local press and then the art sections of the Sydney papers sent journalists to interview us and check out our artists. One in particular was garnering good press coverage after being a finalist in both the annual Wynne and Archibald competitions.

We were so busy that we barely had time to eat and had both lost weight. Jess could ill afford to but I felt better for losing the kilos my travelling had deposited on my thighs. We opened on a Thursday and sold four paintings in the next two days, one for a reasonable sum. It was almost enough to pay our champagne bill! We had a steady stream of visitors and although not turning a profit yet we were heading in that direction. We were enjoying ourselves and I barely had time to think about my love life or lack of it.

We received a magnificent arrangement of white lilies on opening day from Victor and Daphne with a card that wished us luck and a postscript for me that said, "Don't become too busy to hear that knocking at the door, sometimes it is very quiet." I pocketed the card and thought of Christian. I had forbade him from ringing me and I knew it was the right thing to do but I was still disappointed that he hadn't ignored my advice. I guess I was more forgettable than I thought.

Sophie had arranged a couple of dinner parties with eligible men and I had even consented to a few dates. They were all perfectly nice men and I quite enjoyed myself but no bells rang and the whole thing just didn't seem worth the effort. A customer had asked me out. He was almost ten years younger and very good looking and I went out with him because I was so flattered that he had even asked me. He was a music journalist with a long fringe, soulful brown eyes and long elegant fingers. His jeans sat low on his hips and he wore rubber thongs. We had a drink in a bar by the beach and talked about music. He told me about this wonderful new Australian band whose single was 'dynamite'.

"What are they called?" I asked trying to draw my gaze from his pretty eyes.

"*The Cards.* They did this amazing performance at a festival in L.A." He said as he started unknowingly humming their song.

"I was there." I boasted, hoping my street-cred would impress him.

"That is so cool."

"Actually the lead singer is my son." I said proudly.

"Could you get me an interview?" He asked immediately as he looked at me through new eyes.

"Possibly. They are coming back in a few months. Perhaps I could arrange something then"

"Thanks. That would be great ... Julia can I ask you something else?"

I nodded.

"How old are you actually?" I could hear my toy boy fantasy evaporate with each syllable that left his beautiful young mouth.

"Not that I care—I really like older women." He reassured.

As cute as he was I did not think I was ready to be his Demi Moore.

I promised to ask Josh about an interview and he promised to call into the gallery again soon to have a second look at a large abstract painting that appealed to him. We parted company warmed by our mutually beneficial relationship.

Business picked up dramatically in the next few weeks and one customer who had recently moved into the area bought four paintings by one artist. The customer was an American from San Francisco who had been transferred here with her husband for four years. The company had given them an allowance to spend on decorating and happily for us she was choosing to spend it on art. We had recently started showing works by an artist recently returned from Queensland. She painted wonderful landscapes and seascapes but she had also cornered a niche market in modern still life oils. Instead of dead pheasants and dusty fruit bowls she painted kitchen still life; pears sitting upright on a distressed pine dresser and hurriedly unpacked herbs and vegetables spilling onto a kitchen bench. Her work was light, bright, cheery and very affordable and was walking out the door. It was yet another mutually beneficial relationship.

26

THERE WAS AN AUTUMN CHILL in the air when I threw back the doona next morning. I padded out to the kitchen to switch on the kettle. The sky was overcast with rain soaked clouds and the road and sand looked wet from an early morning shower. I contemplated going back to bed for half an hour's commune with the doona or switching on the laptop and checking my email but my new joggers looked at me accusingly. So I drained the last of my tea, threw on shorts and a t-shirt and slid my ipod into my pocket for a brisk walk along the wet sand.

My ipod was on shuffle and I was always curious as to which song would greet me first. Robbie William's assured me that he was trying to be a 'better man' and I really wanted to believe him. I was heading south along the beach, the newly risen sun was climbing slowly on my left and there were fresh dark storm clouds rolling in ahead of me. The sun glinted on the surface of the water while the waves looked diamond green as if lit from underneath as they rose to a white capped peak then crashed noisily onto the sand.

I was on automatic pilot, one foot after the other in syncopated rhythm to the music. The beach was always busy, runners jogging along the beach singly or in pairs, surfers scanning the waves to find the best breaks and today was no exception. I kept checking the progress of the waves so I could run along the firm wet sand without getting my new joggers wet. I made a hurried jump further up the beach to avoid a wave that was breaking closer into shore and when I looked back up I saw yet another runner coming towards me.

He was lean, tanned and shirtless. He wore blue and white hibiscus print boardies and a baseball cap. Sunglasses obscured his face. He ran with a loping gait that was achingly familiar. He had sparse golden chest hair and long legs. My heart skipped a beat then as he drew closer my heart beat so rapidly I was forced to stop walking and try to breathe. He was almost along side me when he turned his head and smiled.

He certainly had a great smile, a smile to turn a woman's head. But there was no dimple. No indentation left by nature's gentle touch.

I felt foolish that I had been so easily fooled and angry with myself for the surge of hope that had coursed through me. I was a busy middle-aged woman with an exciting new business and an interesting life and I had to put a stop to these moments of adolescent indulgence. I simply had to get over Christian.

It was Jess' turn to open the gallery so I had a morning to myself. I ate breakfast standing in the kitchen and trying not to think about Christian. I put on a load of washing and opened my laptop to check for messages from Rebecca and Josh.

Josh had emailed me some photos taken at a shopping mall during a promo visit. There were a few hundred screaming fans, most of them female and the band looked both pumped and shell-shocked. Their single was now on the radio here and I was getting phone-calls from old friends asking if Josh from *The Cards* was really my Josh.

Rebecca had finished Madeline's jewellery and was waiting for Madeline's cousin to come and collect in when he next came to New York. She was still enjoying her course but finding the ice and snow of a New York winter increasingly hard to take. They were both looking forward to a visit home.

The next email in my inbox was unexpected.

> Julia, I hope you don't mind me contacting you but the fact that you gave me your email leads me to hope that you won't be averse to hearing from me. Rebecca may have mentioned that I have been offered a one year guest lectureship at ANU in Canberra. I will be taking up the position after the Easter break but hope to spend a week in Sydney first.
>
> If you have any free time I would love to catch up. Perhaps you can show me the cultural equivalent of a Halloween ball? Do hope you have kept the costume!
>
> I was surprised to hear that you were back in Sydney. Does that mean things with your Englishman did not work out? For your sake I hope that is not the case but my selfishness also hopes that you may now be dating again (particularly middle-aged American art lecturers). Looking forward very much to hearing from you.
>
> Regards, Robert.

I casually mentioned the email to Jess and asked her what she thought.

"Is he the hunk in that Halloween photo?" She asked.

"That's him." I answered

"So let me clarify, Julia," she said ticking off a finger one at a time.

"One, you are single; two, a great looking single guy who you obviously have much in common with wants to see you; three, it is your responsibility as a cultural ambassador for your country to be hospitable and show him around Sydney; and four, he is over thirty." She added pointedly and holding up her last finger.

I remembered how easily we had talked and the kiss he had surprised me with at the hotel room door. Perhaps a weekend spent showing Robert the Sydney sights would be quite fun. Jess was right it was almost my duty to do it and with any luck it would banish the unbidden thoughts of Christian from my head. I would value his opinions on the gallery and he was a very good looking man. There are a lot worse ways to spend time so I emailed back that I had some free time and was looking forward to seeing him.

The university had stepped in however and altered Robert's schedule and he was whisked away to Canberra before he had a chance to see Sydney. I believe it was done with calculating intent; if he was allowed to see Sydney first he would have been unwilling to bury himself in Canberra. I'm sure they lose a lot of foreign academics that way. I'm surprised that they don't black out the car windows until they have passed the outskirts of the city. Despite this he was apparently settling in quite well and the students and staff had been very welcoming. Reading between the lines of his emails though I felt that he was still waiting for our nation's capital to open!

Next weekend however he was finally coming to Sydney. He was yet to brave driving on the wrong side of the road but as I kept reassuring him if he could drive in New York he could drive anywhere. I offered to meet him at the airport but he said he would check into his hotel first and then ring me. I thought for a brief moment of offering him my spare bedroom but it felt too intimate for someone I did not really know that well. Jess was no help at all. She would have had him in my bed at least four weeks ago.

We arranged to meet in the hotel lobby on Friday night and he had booked a restaurant that had been recommended by a colleague. If I felt comfortable with him I would invite him to see the gallery on Saturday.

I felt nervous as I ransacked my wardrobe for something to wear. Should I go for sophisticated art gallery owner in pearls and little black dress or should I try for a more casual Sydney look. As it turned out my worries were pointless as the day at the gallery had been so busy I barely had time for a shower and I grabbed one of the few garments that did not need ironing. I slipped a jersey wraparound dress on, put my, no time to wash hair, in a haphazard twist and spritzed on some perfume. My makeup I could do in the cab.

Robert was sitting at the bar waiting for me. His hair was cut shorter and his face was tanned. He was wearing a beautifully cut dark blue shirt that accentuated a trim waist. His jeans looked like

Armani. His jacket was folded on the stool next to him. He stood when he saw me and moved his jacket to let me sit down.

"I thought I had better reserve you a seat. It's been a challenge fighting off so many beautiful Sydney women though."

His smile was as large as ever. He looked very good and had lost the academic air he wore in New York. I think Australia was agreeing with him.

The conversation flowed as freely as it had before and I was enjoying myself. He was full of questions about Australian customs and idiosyncrasies, most of which I took delight in explaining. I assured him that being called "Robbo" was a compliment, a sign of acceptance but I was unable to offer a rational explanation as to why Aussies added "O" to the end of name when they liked someone.

The meal was wonderful—Asian- Australian fusion cooking at its best. I felt proud of my city and its fresh seafood and varied produce. We drank a Margaret River white and a Hunter Valley dessert wine which he had chosen. I was glad that he appreciated good Australian wines and was adventurous in his palate. I hated wine snobs that judged a wine solely on price.

"Will I get to see your gallery before I have to go back to Canberra?" He asked.

"I could show you in the morning if you like and give you a tour of some of our beaches. We could do the Bondi to Clovelly cliff walk and you can see where the Sculpture by the Sea exhibition is held. Then perhaps a late lunch beside the water somewhere?"

"I could think of nothing I would rather do, especially when I think what the weather is like at home at the moment."

He paid the bill, pulled out my chair and put his arm around my waist as we left the restaurant and started the short walk back to his hotel.

"You've said nothing about your Englishman Julia. Should I pry or pretend to know nothing about him."

"Pretending works well for me at the moment. I have had a lovely night and feel happy and mellow and I am happy for that to continue at least till daylight."

"Would I be pushing my luck if I asked you up to my room for a nightcap then?"

"Just nudging it a bit." I hoped my regretful smile softened the blow. "I'll pick you up at 10 am tomorrow. And I may have said I am ready for any valid criticism of the gallery but I was lying. Please just say you like it. You can always list any criticisms in an email later. I deal better with criticism when it is served cold and in writing."

"You are an intriguing woman Julia. Goodnight." He said as he helped me in to the taxi. He watched the taxi drive away and I wondered what he was really thinking.

Saturday was a glorious Autumn day, warm enough for shirt sleeves but with a hint of freshness in the air and no humidity. I collected Robert as promised and took him directly to the gallery. Jess was there ahead of me looking as gorgeous as ever in tailored black trousers and a camel-coloured silk shirt. She looked expensive and every inch the gallery owner. She charmed Robert and gave him the tour that I was too nervous to conduct. I kept busy in the kitchen making espresso and telling myself that I really did not care what he thought.

My fears were groundless. A smile split his face as he found his way to the kitchen. Jess's eyes were alight with pleasure so I rightly assumed we had passed muster.

"It's sensational Julia. Congratulations. The setting is stunning and there is some real talent gracing your walls. I had no idea you featured ceramic artists as well. Actually there is a piece I would love to purchase for my Canberra flat."

I tried to appear nonchalant but his enthusiastic approval thrilled me, so much so that I sold him the ceramic vase he admired without the commission that Jess usually and rigidly insisted upon. I think she had fallen a little bit in love with Robert and they even found they had some friends in common in New York.

She took me aside to tell me that he had her 100% approval.

"He is the total package Julia. Smart, good looking and he obviously likes you. You have my blessing my child" She said making the sign of the cross over me. "So go off and enjoy yourself. Show him our beautiful city at its best."

"Thankyou Reverend Mother. Are you sure you can handle the crowd on your own." I said as a solitary customer walked through the door.

"I think I can just about manage. Seriously though Julia, go and enjoy yourself, he is a nice man. Just enjoy the moment."

As she spoke the nice man in question came looking for me.

We soon settled into a pattern that suited us both. I spent some weekends in Canberra when he needed a date for an academic function and whenever he could he escaped to Sydney. By the second trip he started to stay at my apartment. We slept together occasionally and it was nice. Nice sex with a nice man. No bells, no choirs of angels just nice.

It was good having an escort for dinner parties and gallery showings. His conversation was stimulating and I learnt much about the art world. With his tutelage I refined my artistic eye and I instilled in him an appreciation for Australian history and wide open spaces.

Jess and her husband were hosting a dinner party to celebrate the success of the gallery's first six months. We had ended the financial year not in the red as I had feared but very firmly in the black—a coup for any gallery but especially for one so new. I liked to think this was due to my artistic vision but knew that it owed more to Jess's keen business sense. Robert was driving up from Canberra for the weekend and I was excited about the party.

Jess is a brilliant hostess and Dave is equally charming with a dry sense of humour. Their house was ultra modern on three levels with ocean views. The walls were off- white and there was lots of glass, marble and stainless steel. Unlike my apartment it was devoid of clutter but it still radiated warmth due to myriad arrangements of flowers and carefully placed art works and curios from their travels.

The dining table was set with heirloom linen and modern crystal and a centrepiece of white lilies. Dave looked very sophisticated in black pants and black shirt although the VB in a stubby holder he held in his left hand was probably a truer indicator of his natural state. I had made the mistake of telling him about Robert's unease with nicknames so should have predicted his response. We walked in the door and Dave gave me a surreptitious wink, held out his hand pumped Robert's hand vigorously and said,

"Robbo, mate, good to finally meet you. Can I get you a beer?"

Jess dug her elbow sharply into his ribs then kissed Robert and I on both cheeks.

"I have to overdo the European customs to balance him out." She said.

We were among the first to arrive so I asked Jess if she minded if I gave Robert a tour of the house. He was suitably impressed. We were making our way back to the dining room when he stopped before a framed photo on the wall of Jess's study.

It had been taken about five years ago and showed Jess, me, Zoe and Sophie all dressed in floaty summer dresses and wearing hats. We were holding glasses of champagne and hamming it up for the camera. We each had a copy of the photo although mine was in an album.

"You look beautiful. I like you in a hat. Was it a wedding?" He asked.

"No, it was Melbourne Cup."

"Oh, I see, you were at the track." He said nodding.

"No, we weren't actually at the track. We were at Sophie's house." I explained.

"But I thought you said it was a Melbourne Cup photo." He asked in confusion.

"It was. We were at Sophie's house, just the girls, watching the race on TV." I tried to explain.

"You were wearing hats and watching television?" He asked with befuddlement.

"Yes. It was Melbourne Cup."

I guess Robert's familiarity with Australian cultural practices had a long way yet to go.

I introduced Robert to the other dinner guests and went to see if Jess needed any help but like always she had everything under control. I related the story about the Melbourne Cup photo and we laughed together at the absurdity of the custom.

Conversation flowed as freely as the wine and after dessert had been served one of Dave's friends asked us all to name two people, dead or alive, famous or obscure who we would like to invite to a dinner party.

Dave wanted Don Bradman and Shane Warne. Zoe thought Princess Di and Adam Sandler would liven things up. Jess could not go past her one true love, Elvis Presley. Marilyn Monroe and JFK were thrown into the mix while Robert opted for Jackson Pollack and a young Sophia Loren.

It was finally my turn but one name alone came into my head. I tired to think of an artist, a sportsman, an actor even a fictitious character but my mind was well and truly blank. I looked around the table at the familiar waiting faces of my friends. I looked at Robert, at his soulful eyes and expectant smile but at that moment I could barely remember his name. I could see only Christian's face, could think of no name but his. Christian's intrusion into my brain was so overpowering that I could feel tears welling in my eyes. Jess in her intuitive fashion sensed my panic and quickly raised her glass in a toast.

"Here's to continuing success at the gallery and to partnership." She said inclining her head towards me.

Robert looked at me with a question in his eyes that I did my best to ignore.

When we left Jess hugged me tight and whispered in my ear. "Ring me."

Robert and I did not sleep together that night. I suddenly felt like I was cheating, conducting the affair that Christian had accused me of.

I busied myself in the laundry next morning, hand-washing things that I normally threw into the machine. I swept floors, plumped cushions and wiped non-existent crumbs off the bench anything that would keep me from sitting down and talking to Robert. He was packed up and ready to drive back to Canberra by eleven am and I had no more tasks that I could pretend were pressing. I smiled brightly and offered to help him with his bags to the car.

"Stop it Julia and just sit." He demanded as he took my hand and led me back to the kitchen table. "Shall I tell you what you are not saying or do you want to show some maturity and do it yourself?"

I looked into his searching brown eyes but could find no words. The tears spilling down my cheeks probably said it all.

"You are not over him are you? This Englishman of yours still has a hold on your heart."

"I'm sorry." I said trying to wipe the tell-tale tears from my eyes. "I really do not want to feel this way. You deserve more, more than I have been able to give."

I shuddered as I heard myself offer this inadequate relationship cliché .

He reached across the table and took my hands in his. I bent my head and studied our entwined fingers. He had elegant hands and neatly manicured nails. They looked trustworthy and reassuring. They were the sort of hands that could guide a smooth and measured path through life, hands that could caress and console. They were desirable hands but yet the wrong hands. I drew my eyes from their reassuring sight and lifted my head to face his gaze.

"It's okay Julia. We were friends before we were lovers and we can be friends again. I like you very much but I am not a love-struck teenager, nursing a broken heart."

My relief at his resilience assuaged my guilt while deflating my ego.

"What are you going to do about the way you feel? Pretend you don't feel it but yet measure every other man against him and find them wanting?" He asked with just enough venom to make me think he felt more than he admitted.

I could not answer. I had made it plain to Christian that there was no place in my life for him. And it seems that he had taken me at my word. There had been no pleading phone-calls, no tentative emails no toe dipped in the turbulent relationship waters. I imagined him still living with Rhonda, still walking on tiptoes around her. He may still have a hold on my heart but it appeared that his was not yet free to give. Perhaps it never would be. I shrugged my shoulders and said,

"I don't know. I am an idiot and I really am sorry." It sounded lame and immature.

I walked him to his car and he hugged me. I knew I was going to miss his reassuring embrace and the smell of his aftershave. I truly was an idiot. He threw his bag in the boot and slid into the bucket seat. As the engine fired the radio came on preset as usual to classic rock. He turned to me and grimaced as the strains of Crosby, Stills Nash and Young filled the air. They exhorted us to *Love the one you're with.*

Life imitates art at the most inopportune times. We both smiled self-consciously. I stood and watched him drive off and as the car became a blur in the distance I could still hear the song in my head. If only it was that simple.

The next few weeks brought many surprises including a quick visit home from Josh. The band was on a ten a day interview juggernaut to promote the new album. It seemed that every time I changed radio stations I heard his voice. I held true to my promise to my toy boy journalist friend and arranged for him to meet Josh.

Josh was impressed with the gallery and loved the apartment. He managed to spend five nights with me and arrived with enough dirty laundry to keep a laundromat in business for a month. He did not expect me to do it for him of course and as he explained he would have got around to it eventually, but his fans had to come first at this stage of his career. As I washed the twelfth pair of jeans and ironed the twentieth t-shirt I remained unconvinced.

After two days of Josh's company the apartment looked very lived in. There were wet towels on the bed, whiskers in the basin and toothpaste trails on the bathroom vanity. The pantry door was left open, empty milk cartons were returned to the fridge and the lid to the vegemite jar disappeared mysteriously to be found months later on the balcony leading an undercover life as an ashtray. The recycle bin was full of beer bottles and pizza boxes. It was chaotic. Old friends dropped in constantly and a few groupies even gathered and giggled out the front. The walls of the apartment resonated with music and the constant ring of his mobile.

I loved it. Josh's company kept both my mind and body busy with no time for introspection. When he left to return to the States I cried yet again.

A week after his departure I was sitting in the gallery office updating our on-line catalogue and answering emails from our artists. My inbox was teeming and I was ruthlessly deleting when I found an email from Gemma the only woman from my old job with whom I had maintained contact. She often sent me jokes and chain letters which I deleted without reading when pressed for time. This one was titled **"And they say romance is dead!"** The last thing I needed at the moment was to focus on someone else's happy little romance when mine was so soundly kaput.

I opened the message from Gemma prepared to delete the attachment but her message stayed my hand. "**You really should see this it is quite moving Julia. It almost brought a tear to my eye. And you know how seldom that happens. Let's catch up soon. G.**"

There were three attachments. I clicked on the first one and my screen filled with an art work. The work was unfamiliar but the scene was not. Two figures faced a moonlit ocean while giant leatherback turtles lumbered up the sand. The moonlight bathed the painting with a seductive luminescence. Its beauty took my breath away and my heart skipped a beat.

Attachment two was a photo taken through the window of an art gallery. A man in an empty gallery sat looking at the same painting. There were tears pooling in his eyes. It was a very good photo, apparently an award winning photo. My heart was beating so rapidly I feared it would leave my chest.

My hand trembled as I opened attachment three. It was a newspaper article from one of the London Sunday supplements picked up from a local Cornwall newspaper.

> Portrait of an Artist
>
> By Marie Webb
>
> Rodney Jones, this year's recipient of the prestigious Blakely Award for photography provides us with some background on his award winning photograph and its subject, painter Chris Gilham.
>
> R.J"I attended the gallery opening last October for our regional newspaper when I overheard art dealer Nigel Baines ask Mr. Gilham if he could purchase a canvas not listed in the sale catalogue. The canvas titled "Inception" (see facing page) had not been hung for the exhibition. The artist refused to sell, resisting all Baines' entreaties and an extremely generous offer. My curiosity was piqued and even more so when I discovered that it had been painted as

a gift for an unknown woman and no inducement would persuade the artist to sell it."

M.W.How did you capture such an emotive photographic image?

R.J."The gallery had closed and I was packing up my gear and loading the car when I looked back through the lit window. The artist was sitting in the deserted gallery staring at a canvas. My eyes followed his gaze and the previously unhung work was now on the wall. He seemed to be lost to the present and I just captured the moment when the first sign of tears caught in the corner of his eyes."

Rodney's moving image has not only won the Blakely Award but has also captured the imagination of the romantic in us all. Who is this woman who has so captured the artist's heart and why hasn't he presented her with this beautiful gift?

I sat mesmerised by the images before me as a million conflicting thoughts ran helter-skelter through my brain. Jess called out from her desk that there was a phone call for me. I asked her to take a message. I felt too naked to deal with the world at the moment.

She sidled quietly up behind me and looked at the image on the screen.

"Wow! I love the way the moonlight has been captured. One of our prospective artists I hope."

"No." I answered abruptly.

She looked at me strangely and asked softly. "Are you okay?"

"Not really. Do you mind if I head off home? My head feels as if it will explode."

I was almost out the door when she raced after me, message slip in hand. She handed it to me and wrapped her arms around me in a wordless embrace. I could feel tears forcing their way through my resolve. I smiled and thanked her and shoved the message slip into my pocket.

It was hours later when I remembered it. I padded to the laundry and hauled my trousers out of the clothes hamper and felt in the pocket for the scrap of paper. I smoothed it out and moved into a better light to read Jess's familiar untidy scrawl. It was a local phone number but not one I recognised. The name however was very familiar. How surprising.

27

"THIS IS THE FINAL BOARDING CALL for all passengers travelling on flight QF 108 to Sydney. Your plane is ready for departure." He could hear the voice in the background and he knew she had to go but Christian could not make himself end the call. It could not be possible that he had finally found her again for it to end like this.

He convinced himself that if he gave her time and space she would relent and contact him again. But the weeks went by and he heard nothing. He visualised her returning to her home and wondered how she was coping. Had she slotted back into her previous existence or had the long absence made her restless and ill-content with her old life. As winter galloped toward him and the days shortened he thought longingly of balmy summer days walking along the beach and nights spent beside her tangled in sweaty sheets. He became obsessive about checking the daily temperature in Sydney and even reading her star sign in the vain hope that it would provide a clue to her daily life. Christmas came and went and a new year rolled relentlessly on. When he discovered that Madeline and Michael and even Merilyn had received Christmas cards from her it hit him with great force that she was serious about moving on without him.

When Rhonda returned from London she was greeted by her belongings on the porch and an implacable Christian. She sensed that this time he was serious and her usual blackmailing techniques failed to move him. She was strangely relieved. Cheating and scheming were exhausting and Claude was proving to be more than a distraction. He laughed at her attempts to manipulate him and seemed to be able to see the vulnerable self she thought she kept well hidden beneath the lacquer-hard exterior. She found herself softening under his care.

When he asked her to move to Paris she was surprised, pleased and terrified. She had looked upon him as a dalliance to feed her self esteem but somewhere in his embrace she had found a safe harbour instead.

When the Blakely award photograph was published Christian was mortified. He had been unaware when he had signed the release for the gallery photos that this photo was among them. He admitted it was an emotive image but he felt raw and violated by it. Every time that he looked at the painting now fresh waves of embarrassment coursed through his body. It was bad enough when it was just a few locals who smiled at him kindly but when the damn article went national life became unbearable. Bus loads of middle-aged women seemed to pour through the gallery doors daily.

They would wander through the exhibition with their eyes darting sideways like the garishly painted clowns from sideshow alley and whenever he made an appearance he was engulfed in a miasma of excited chatter. The only thing that kept him from shoving coloured balls in their gaping mouths was the desire to avoid further publicity. His days seemed to be accompanied by a soundtrack of communal sighs and understanding smiles.

It did not help that his friends thought it was extremely amusing. Merilyn particularly got the giggles whenever another group of romantically addicted women went into the coffee shop for cake and a slice of gossip. After the umpteenth time that he met her giggles with a scowl she snapped at him and said,

"For God's sake Chris get over yourself. Your business and mine are doing brilliantly because of the publicity. Let the old dears have their mo-

ments of romantic indulgence."

"I might be able to appreciate the romance of it more if the 'mystery woman' they all want to know about wanted anything to do with me." He answered.

"So it is not just about embarrassment and bruised ego then?"

Christian shook his head sadly.

"Have you tried to phone her? Write? Email? Carrier pigeon?" Merilyn asked.

"I have written numerous letters in my head and composed heartfelt phone-calls where I am eloquent and convincing but no, I have not tried to contact her. She was very forceful when she said that we had no future and she did not want to hear from me again."

Merilyn handed Christian the latte she had brought him and said,

"You know how good I am at unsolicited advice so I will not disappoint you now. I saw how Julia was when she was here Chris and she could not hide the fact that she loved you." He started to raise his hand in protest but she continued. "She was hurt Chris, a lot more than I think you realise and she knew that Rhonda was still pulling the strings. She may have said she did not want to hear from you but I guarantee she does. I'm sure every time the phone rings some part of her hopes it is you."

Merilyn's parting words to him had been, "what do you have to lose?" The loss of hope, the loss of possibility; not trying at least prevented him failing again. Perhaps Madeline could offer him some insight. He knew that she had kept in contact and he had so far resisted the impulse to grill her about Julia. Perhaps now was the time to swallow his pride and ask her what she thought. She should know whether Julia had really moved on and found someone else.

The decision made, his heart lifted. A small nugget of hope lodged in his chest and images of a reunion crept into his mind. He drove home excited to tell Max of his decision. Max had long held a candle for Julia and he felt sure that he would bestow an enthusiastic if silent endorsement of his plans. He parked the car and let himself in through the laundry door and listened for the shuffling sound of Max's claws on the timber floors. But the house was silent. He turned on lights and was relieved when he saw the sleeping dog's figure on his bed in front of the fire. He approached and called his name but there was no answering wag of the tail and his ears did not perk up in their usual fashion. He knelt down beside him, wrapped his arms around the still warm body and sobbed.

28

THE PHONE WAS ANSWERED after the third ring by a dispiritingly chirpy hotel receptionist.

"Can you put me through to Madeline Maurier please." I asked, trying yet failing to match her chirpy tones.

She had barely said, "certainly" before I heard Madeline's voice ask with an uncharacteristic girlish giggle.

"Bonsoir Julia. Are you surprised?"

"Stunned. What are you doing in Sydney? How long are you here for?"

"I'm attending a conference with the bank for four days. I was a last minute choice after a colleague fell ill or I would have let you know."

"You have some free time to get together I hope?"

"Tomorrow's seminar finishes quite early and there is no dinner planned. I should be free by about 4pm, would that suit you?" She suggested.

"It would be perfect. I have so many questions ... about the wedding plans and Michael. How about coming here? That way we can talk to our heart's content without interruption."

I knew well the impact Madeline made as she walked into a room and I did not want the distraction of the admiration of male eyes and the envy of female ones. I wanted her company to myself. I gave her the address and she said she would organise a taxi through the concierge.

She arrived promptly on the doorstep at 4pm and looked even more beautiful than I had remembered. Her hair had grown out of its geometrical cut and was softer around her face. She had changed out of corporate attire into skinny dark jeans and tan high-heeled boots and a gorgeous cowl neck sweater in the softest gum-leaf green cashmere.

Her arms were laden with gifts and photos. I put her bottle of Bollinger in ice to chill and the enormous bunch of yellow roses needed two vases to contain them. Madeline expressed her admiration for the apartment and my growing art collection and as I watched her move around the room I envied yet again her elegance of movement. I made coffee and we sat on the lounge to talk.

By the time dinner was finished every topic was exhausted and neither of us had as yet mentioned Christian's name. I could hold off no longer.

"How is he?" I asked searching her face for a hint of the answer before she uttered a word.

"The gallery is doing really well but he seems a little lost and lonely. And when Max died we were really worried about him..."

"Max died?" I interjected. "Oh, poor Christian, he loved him so much he must have been devastated." I found my cheeks wet with unbidden tears. Max had been such a large part of his life for so long. The thought of no companion for his long walks along the estuary, no boisterous greeting when his key turned in the lock left me feeling empty and useless. Max and I had shared many secrets also – those long velvety ears had been as accepting of confidences as they had petting.

" Rhonda, ... was she understanding?" I asked. A fleeting look of surprise crossed Madeline's face.

"Rhonda lives in Paris now Julia. I assumed that you knew. She is living with my uncle Claude and against all predictions they seem really happy. He does not tolerate her attempts at manipulation and when she tries to make him feel guilty about some imagined misdemeanour he just laughs and kisses the top of her head. He never tries to reason with her he just does what he wants and tells her she is adorable. We are all so surprised and Michael says he has never seen his mother this content."

"So she left Christian again then did she?"

"No, not at all. Christian made the move this time. He packed her belongings and left them at the door. He would not even let her step over the threshold. When he found out what part she had played in breaking you two up he was so angry I think he could easily have killed her."

So he had been telling me the truth about Rhonda and his mobile phone. Maybe I had been too quick in my refusal to listen to his pleas. But if Rhonda was really out of his life why hadn't he tried to contact me. I debated whether to ask Madeline but she saved me the decision.

"He wanted to call you after Max died. He asked me whether he should ring you. But Rebecca had told me that you had been seeing her art professor and seemed happy. I did not know what to advise. I thought you would want to know about Max but I did not know how serious your relationship was. So that is what I told him. So I assume he did not ring?"

What must he think of me. He must believe that I had lied to him about Robert all along.

"No, he did not ring. Robert and I were really just friends who dated occasionally. I was never in love with him. We parted company months ago." I explained to her and tried to convince myself that it had been as simple as I said.

A transfiguring smile lit her face and she reached into the Chloe handbag that I had been covetously admiring all evening and handed me an envelope of fine ecru linen.

"I was going to give you this anyway but now I can do it with greater pleasure."

I opened the envelope and looked at her with surprise.

"It's a wedding invitation, your wedding invitation and it is in Paris." I said with great facility at stating the obvious. She laughed and said, "I know."

A thousand thought raced through my brain. Can I afford to go? It's Paris, a wedding in Paris. It's romance personified. My thoughts then skidded to a roadblock of mammoth proportions. What about Christian? What about Rhonda?

"I am flattered by the invitation Madeline and you know I would love to be there but I couldn't embarrass Christian or even Rhonda like that. There are enough dramas on a wedding day without manufacturing more." I said sadly.

"Sometimes you can be very dense Julia. Who do you think insisted I invite you? Who has been plaguing me to find out if you were indeed in love with someone else?"

"He did? He wants me there even with Rhonda there? "

"He wants you there and so do Michael and I. Please say you can come."

Next day at the gallery I relayed the conversation to Jess.

"What would she have done if you were still seeing Robert?" Jess asked.

"I asked Madeline that and she said she was to invite us both and Christian would just have to deal with it. Do you think it means that he is still interested?"

"Madeline's right Julia you are dense! Of course he is interested—you only have to look at that infamous painting to know that. Now tell me that you are going. I can easily manage for a couple of weeks without you."

The gallery had recently received a huge boost when we were asked to source art works for a merchant bank with money to burn. Jess's contacts in the corporate world and her marketing skills were insuring that we stayed decidedly in the black. This commission alone was worth five figures to us so I could afford to go to the wedding if I wanted and I wanted very much indeed.

I didn't know what would happen or even what I wanted to happen but I did not want our last contact to be the angry words we had last exchanged. I sent a wedding acceptance to Madeline and Michael and I composed a hand-written note to Christian in which I expressed my sympathy for his loss. I read it through again then tore it up. I enclosed instead a photo I had taken of Max. His ears were flying and his tongue lolling as he futilely and joyously chased a rabbit through the spinifex grass. The sun was setting and the scene was bathed in a soft amber glow. I held the photo in my hand and I could almost feel the last warm rays of the sun and could hear Max's panting intermingled with our laughter. I hurriedly scribbled on the back. ***I'm sure the rabbits are easier to catch in dog heaven! I'm sorry Christian, with love Julia.*** Would he be able to read between the lines?

Jess told me I was mad and should just ring him but I needed to see his face. I needed to look into his eyes to see the truth of his feelings. There had been too much misunderstanding and misinformation. This time I was not going to script his responses ahead of time. This time I was not giving in to imaginary romantic scenarios—well maybe just a little bit and only after a glass or two of wine when listening to love songs. But apart from that minor lapse I would be rational and sensible.

29

MY SEATBELT WAS BUCKLED low and tight, my tray table was in the upright position and my hand luggage was securely stowed. The flight attendant had failed to give any instruction for the stowage of emotional baggage and I believed this to be a serious oversight.

In the interest of aviation safety please refrain from crying in the toilets; all conjecture about the future should be switched off for the duration of the flight and any problems left behind at your departure can be reclaimed at the emotional baggage carousel on your arrival. Now sit back and enjoy your flight.

I had doubted whether I would ever make the flight and as it was I was leaving four days later than I had originally planned. I had wanted to be in Paris days before the wedding so I could buy a dress from a boutique off the Rue de Rivoli that Jess said was fabulous. They specialised in designer gowns at ridiculously reduced prices which equated to only about five times more expensive than anything I owned. I knew it was morally wrong and immature to try and compete with the mother of the groom but what the hell I would confess and grow up later.

I had intended to be in Paris early enough to meet Christian ahead of time but now I would barely have time to shower and dress before the ceremony and then only if there were no delays on the flight. Jess had come through like the angel of mercy that she is by loaning me her brand new Alex Perry dress, bought to wear to a ritzy charity dinner. I had no idea that it was possible to feel such lust for a dress and a shower of tingling ran from my fingertips to my toes when I thought of it.

It was a perfect ballerina length concoction of layers of the finest tulle overlaid by ivory satin and an apron of delicate black scalloped lace which ended about thirty centimetres above the hemline. The bodice of the same fine lace had a deep V- neckline front and back and the cinched in waist was dressed with a black satin sash. The dress managed to showcase the waist, legs and cleavage all in one – it was an engineering marvel. I was paranoid about losing it so had brought it on board as hand luggage in a garment bag. Hopefully it would bounce back into shape with a good shake once released from its necessary imprisonment.

Jess had driven me to the airport, kissed me goodbye and assured me that she could cope with insurance companies and builders in my absence. The day before my planned departure Sydney had turned on one of her violent havoc-wreaking hail storms. My beautiful city was like an angelically placid child most of the time but when she felt her residents were taking her beauty for granted she threw tantrums of stupendous proportions.

It had been an unseasonably hot September day, a foretaste of summer sent to tease us. The beach was packed and people had been wandering in and out of the gallery all day. We were just preparing to close when the sky suddenly darkened to a deep murky green and a roar like a freight train on steroids rolled towards us. Beachgoers stopped and looked skywards as if searching for UFOs, then it hit. Hail stones the size of golf balls, many as big as cricket balls rained down like artillery fire. People screamed and tried to protect their heads as blood trickled down their faces. Beach-goers pushed into the gallery seeking shelter as we tried desperately to remove paintings from the walls and move them to the back of the gallery. Ten minutes later it was all over, the sun was shining benignly again as residents and visitors numbly surveyed the damage.

It was like an improbable snow-dome scene, palm trees shredded and surrounded by a carpet of white snow, surfers holding pockmarked surfboards and shaking their heads. Every window in the gallery was shattered and many of the roof tiles but when we caught our breath and surveyed the damage the majority of our paintings had escaped serious damage. The work that had been showcased in the window though now resembled a colander. I thought it was an improvement and suggested we pass it off as the latest avant-garde technique but judging by the raised eyebrows my suggestion engendered I assumed nobody else agreed.

The SES rescue teams did what they could but with nowhere to store the paintings, no windows and no alarm system we were forced to sleep at the gallery until the insurance company could organise a glazier. I could not leave Jess on her own to fend off possible marauding hordes, so I rebooked my flight and spent three nights camping on the gallery floor. The leg wax, facial and spray tan I had booked for the next morning became a quick leg shave, an exfoliating shower and an acceptance of the allure of pale skin. At least I had Cinderella's dress.

I still had not spoken to Christian although he had finally joined the technological revolution and emailed me. He thanked me for the photo and we exchanged polite enquiries from one business owner to another. It was civilised, proper and noncommittal. He booked me into the Hotel Bel Ami off the Boulevard St. Germaine which he said was walking distance to the church. He neglected to say if he was staying there also and I politely neglected to ask. It was as though we both needed the physical presence of the other to engage in meaningful communication.

My last visit to Paris had been conducted at supersonic speed and Steve and I had only two days there but even with such a brief glimpse I had loved it. I was excited about seeing it again. I remembered walking along the Seine at dusk hand in hand watching the lights come on one by one, the house-boats illuminated and gifting a glimpse of another life to passers-by. He had squeezed my hand and said that we would come back. I promise, he said. I t was the only promise he had made throughout our marriage that he had failed to keep.

The taxi dropped me at the hotel by eleven in the morning and my room was not yet ready. I longed to strip off my clothes and soak in a tub for an hour then slide between cool hotel sheets for a nap but I had not slept much on the flight and feared that if I crept into bed I would not wake up in time for the wedding. So I convinced myself that it was fortunate that I would have to wait for my room.

The clerk took care of my luggage but I was still reluctant to hand over my dress and the garment bag appeared to be expanding, all that tulle was obviously plotting an escape. I started to walk out of the hotel to find a café for a coffee and croissant when the clerk called after me.

"Excusez- moi Madame I almost forgot, I have a message for you." He handed me a folded message slip which asked me to call at room 423 when I arrived. There was no name on the message.

"Excuse me monsieur, do you know who the message is from?"

"No, madame. I have just come on duty and the message was already here."

I assumed it must have been Christian but it seemed odd that he had not left a more personal message. Well, only one way to find out. I took the lift to the fourth floor, still ridiculously clutching my dress and found room 423. I knocked tentatively and debated whether my jet-lagged body would enable me to flee if the room's occupant happened to be an axe-murderer or French serial killer. The leap to such a macabre thought was obviously fuelled by jetlag.

The door opened slowly and a woman jumped from behind it and yelled "Surprise!" I screamed, dropped my dress and turned to run when my slowly functioning brain convinced me to turn around. There in the doorway with her arms open wide was Rebecca.

"Mum, I'm sorry I did not mean to scare you. I just wanted to surprise you."

We hugged and then hugged again and Rebecca said, "I asked Madeline not to tell you that she had invited me. I was hoping it would be a nice surprise."

"It is a nice surprise Bec and when my heart rate approaches something more normal I will appreciate it even more." I turned her around so I could get a better look at her. Her hair was dark now with a heavy fringe, very different from the blonde waves I had last seen. "I like the hair, you look quite European and sophisticated."

"I'm just trying it out for a while but I am not sure it is really me." She said looking at her reflection in the mirror and pulling faces.

"What's with the garment bag? You're clutching it like it contains the crown jewels." She asked.

"Almost," I replied, "it's an Alex Perry dress on loan from Jess." I explained the whole gallery damage and delay debacle and she was suitably concerned. "You know," I said, looking around her spacious double room, "perhaps I can cancel my room and we can share?"

She hesitated for a moment then a slight blush inflamed her cheeks as it had always done as a child when she was placed into an awkward situation. I took another look around the room and noticed things that had escaped my attention before. There were two suitcases open in the corner and a pair of reading glasses on the bedside table sitting atop a novel that appeared to be in French. There were two used coffee cups on the table and a furtive glimpse into the bathroom showed shaving cream and a razor. I knew that Bec was a girl who waxed not shaved and slowly all these observations filtered into my brain.

"You're not alone." I said

"I'm not alone." She said at the same time.

I raised my eyebrows in inquiry and said, "Tell me more ..." when we both turned at the sound of a key in the door. Rebecca leapt to her feet, took the hand of the young man who had just entered and drew him further into the room. He was about twenty-five, slight in build and of a little above average height. He had a firm jaw-line, well defined cheek-bones and silken dark hair that fell onto his face. In fact he looked a lot like Madeline—he even moved with her same economy of movement.

He held out his hand then thought better of it and kissed me on both cheeks.

"Bonjour, I am Jean Coty. Rebecca has told me about you

Madame Kennedy and it is mon plaisir to meet you." He said in a tangled mix of French and English.

I turned to Rebecca and said, "Don't you think Jean bears a resemblance to Madeline?"

They looked at one another and smiled.

"That is because Jean is Madeline's cousin. He came to New York on business and offered to collect her jewellery. He ended up staying a little longer than expected." Rebecca looked up at Jean with love stamped all over her face and my heart did a little somersault. Anxiety and joy competed for dominance but I gave joy the upper hand, this was Paris after all.

They detailed for me the history of their romance and I felt relieved that Jean obviously reflected Rebecca's feelings. First an uncle for Rhonda now a cousin for Rebecca perhaps there was a niece for Josh secreted away somewhere. Madeline's family could run their own dating agency judging by their success rate.

I looked at my watch and suggested that I check to see if my room was ready yet as we would need to leave for the wedding in a few hours. They both looked at me strangely.

"The wedding is on Saturday mum, not today," said a perplexed Rebecca.

"But today is Saturday. I left Sydney on Friday and flew for a few hundred hours so it must be Sat ... Oh, I forgot that whole international dateline thing didn't I?"

Well at least I would have time to shake out the dress and have a night's sleep. It was well worth looking like an idiot for such unexpected luxuries.

Jean went down to reception and collected my key and escorted me to my room. He opened the door for me and hesitated for a moment before he spoke.

"Rebecca, she is special to me and I would like you to know."

"Thankyou, Jean. I appreciate you telling me." I said and kissed him on just one cheek attempting to hold on to some Australian heritage.

They promised to collect me at seven tonight and take me to dinner in the Latin Quarter.

I took the longed for bath and slipped between the pristine sheets for a brief nap wondering if I would see Christian before tomorrow but as tired as I was I could not quieten my brain.

What if Rhonda causes a scene when she sees me and we ruin the wedding? What if when Christian and I finally see one another again the spark is gone? What will happen between Rebecca and Jean, will it end in heartbreak? Is it wrong to be in Paris without Steve? Do Christian and I really love one another – and is love enough to make it work?

Was it unfair to Jess to leave her with all the mess of our shared business? Has worrying about something ever prevented it from happening? The only question I could answer with certainty was the last one.

I was convinced that I had not really closed my eyes but when I checked the clock it was three hours later and time to get ready for dinner.

Paris by twilight was as magical as I had remembered and the walk in the cool air finally chased away the cobwebs in my cluttered head. It genuinely was a city of love and couples strolled everywhere hand in hand. We passed pavement cafes where lovers exchanged kisses over their aperitifs and long lingering embraces at apartment doors. Even in the Metro the leave-taking to jump on a local train and head home was heralded by the sort of goodbye that Aussies save for troops heading off to war.

The women were simply and elegantly dressed in neutral tones and classic styles. A sensational handbag or quirkily knotted scarf added colour and individuality to the simplest outfit. Even the tourists were better dressed in Paris as though the city held them up to a new standard.

Over dinner I had the opportunity to observe Jean at close quarters and I liked what I saw. He was attentive to Rebecca and me also but without an over abundance of Gallic show. His good manners seemed natural and his English was fluent after his nervousness subsided. He was also extremely amusing which is difficult in another language. Jean explained that there was a rehearsal dinner tonight for the wedding party and the parents so that explained Christian's whereabouts. We shared a bottle of Chablis and plates of African food and Jean told me of the history of the church where the wedding was to take place.

"The church is just a few minutes walk from our hotel," Jean said as a slight blush infused his face as we both thought of that double bed in Rebecca's room, "it is along the Boulevard Saint- Germain in Place St. Germain Des Pres. It is the oldest church in Paris and Madeline's family church." He said with pride.

"How old is it Jean and remember anything over two hundred years is old to an Australian?" I asked

He laughed and answered, "It was built by the Merovingian King Childebert in 542 but the Normans destroyed the Abbey in the 9th Century and the church was then enlarged and consecrated by Pope Alexander III in about 1163. It has a wonderful Romanesque interior and some frescoes from the 19th Century." He looked embarrassed and said,

"I'm sorry, I did not mean to bore you."

Rebecca squeezed his hand and said, "You didn't, Mum loves history even more than I do. I still find it hard to comprehend the age of all the monuments and buildings in Paris. Some times the past seems more real than the present and when I turn a corner I expect to see robed monks and medieval peasants."

"Imagine how many marriages must have been consecrated there over the centuries. Lots of them just business and political arrangements too I suppose." I said thinking sadly of young brides bartered away to older husbands to secure a family's wealth or standing.

"Not this one at least," asserted Rebecca, "I have never seen two people more in love than Michael and Madeline. I can't wait until tomorrow to see the bride."

"And to see the exquisite artwork you created for her worn in a setting to match its beauty." Jean added and this time it was Rebecca's turn to blush.

We strolled leisurely back to the hotel and I knew what Rebecca meant. The past and the present merged into the continuum of time. Perhaps my past with Christian and the present and future were all part of the same fabric. My musings or as they probably should have been called, jet-lagged induced philosophy 101, at least ensured a sound night's sleep.

The day of the wedding shone bright and clear with a cloudless cobalt sky. I spent the morning at the Musee d'Orsay losing myself amongst my favourite Impressionist painters and was stunned anew by the beauty that surrounds us. I walked back along the Seine and smiled at those I passed. I was too nervous to eat lunch and I did not want to add extra strain to the waistband of my dress.

I showered and slipped into the dress and it did not disappoint, it truly was a marvel. I did a few twirls around the hotel room and looked at myself from every angle. I looked good and said a silent prayer to both Alex Perry and Jess. I did my hair into a French twist (when in Rome etc.) and it also looked good. A great dress and a good hair day what could possibly go wrong?

I found out soon enough when I took my black stilettos from my bag. There were two black high heels both with discreet bows at the peep toes, one with a three inch heel and one with a five inch heel. I threw my mind back to my frenzied packing and I could see both pairs on the bed as I tried to decide which pair to pack. I now had a foot in both camps! It was unlikely the wedding service and reception would be conducted on a slope of 45 degrees so I had to find some other shoes. Rebecca took two sizes larger than me so she could not help. I could not wear my red ballet flats or my Nikes or boots I would have to go and buy some.

I rang Rebecca and Jean and told them to go on without me and I would catch up. I tore the dress off and threw myself back into the jeans I had just discarded and raced off to the shoe shops I had seen on my walk back from the museum. What had seemed like a brief stroll was in fact a twenty minute jog as I forced my way rudely through idling shoppers and tourists. I bought the only pair that I tried on from the first shop that I saw. They were ridiculously expensive but thankfully sensational. By the time I got back to the hotel I was sweaty and starting to get a headache. I had to shower again and throw down two paracetamol before I could slide back into Cinderella's dress. I tidied my hair, touched up my make, applied a liberal dose of Dior Cherie and raced out the door and walked the two blocks to the church as quickly as new $500 stilettos would allow and arrived just as the bride's car was pulling up.

30

I raced up the stairs to the church entrance and paused as I tried to quieten my racing heart. There were massed displays of white lilies and roses overflowing from the vases adorning the altar and the candlelight was throwing shadows onto the stained glass windows and competing for dominance with the late afternoon sun filtering through them.

I hesitantly started the walk down the aisle questioning again if I was making the right decision. I raised my eyes to the altar and saw him. "Please turn," I begged and he turned his head as if in answer to my unvoiced prayer. He saw me and an eye-creasing smile lit his face. It was a smile that breathed life into his face and started to melt my doubts.

I slid into the pew beside Rebecca and Jean as discretely as I could and we all turned to watch the bride's progression down the aisle. She was breathtaking. Her simple ivory satin dress was almost Edwardian in style and with her heirloom lace veil and circlet of fresh flowers she could have stepped out of the pages of a history book. The necklace and earrings that Rebecca had created for her were stunning in their simplicity – an elegant tracery of pearls set in gold.

When the service finished my heart started to race again as Christian walked towards me. I had never seen him in a dinner suit in fact I had never seen him in a suit at all. He looked very James Bond in his Armani and I fully expected to see a martini in one hand and a gun in the other. He leaned in and kissed me on the cheek and I introduced him to Rebecca and Jean.

"I'm so happy that you came." He took my hand in his and said, "You look beautiful Julia." The touch of his hand sent shivers down my arm and into other places it was inappropriate to mention in church. We watched the bridal party return from signing the Marriage certificate and Michael turned and caught his father's eye.

"They are happy aren't they ... I mean with one another, not just today?" He asked as a look of sudden doubt fought for a place on his smiling face.

"They're happy and right for one another Christian." I reassured and he squeezed my hand in response. The photographer was beckoning to him.

"Time for more happy snaps it seems. Will you wait for me out in front?"

He walked quickly down the aisle and I watched his progress. Rebecca leant in and said out of Jean's hearing,

"Tasty mum, very tasty." And now it was my turn to blush.

We made our way to the front of the church and watched the photographer position the group for shots in front of the gothic tower. Tourists were stopping to photograph the church and join in the moment. Jean took Rebecca off to meet some of his friends and family and I was left on my own to observe.

I had to reluctantly admit that Rhonda looked sensational in a coffee coloured lace dress. She looked prettier than I had remembered perhaps that is what happiness does to you. I congratulated the bride and groom and turned to find Christian at my side. He introduced me to Madeline's parents who both said they had heard much of me from their daughter.

"There is someone else I want you to meet," he said as he took my hand firmly in his and lead me towards Rhonda and a distinguished looking man I assumed was Claude.

"Rhonda, Claude, I would like you to meet Julia Kennedy."

Claude did the Gallic kiss on both cheeks and Rhonda shook my proffered hand. As Claude engaged Christian in conversation Rhonda moved close to me and said,

"I believe I owe you an apology Julia. If I am responsible for ruining you affair with Chris I am sorry. Maybe you can make him happy, God knows I never could." She turned a proprietary eye toward the talking men and I was not convinced that she didn't still think she owned them both but I accepted her apology in the sentiment with which it was offered.

It was a wonderful wedding—the champagne flowed freely, the food was exquisite and Christian and I danced together for the first time. It shocked me when I realised this and I was forced to accept how little time we had actually spent together – the eight weeks in Southeast Asia twenty-five years ago and the intense four weeks in Cornwall a year ago. We really knew so little about one another's lives. I knew nothing about his previous relationships apart from Rhonda, nothing about his medical history, his favourite movies. Did he have any allergies? How often did he get his hair cut, his teeth cleaned? Should I ask him these things?

As he waltzed me around the room and my perfect dress twirled out around me I caught a surreptitious glance from Rhonda. She moved closer to Claude and put her hand over his in a gesture of ownership and smiled at me. The smile did not quite reach her eyes but I could tell it was trying to. Christian drew me back into his embrace as the music stopped and I found myself saying,

"How often do you go to the dentist?"

He put his hand over his mouth self-consciously and said quietly,

"Have I got something stuck in my teeth?"

"No. I'm sorry—I just thought it was something I should know." I knew I sounded ridiculous.

"Here, now, you thought it was important?" He asked incredulously.

"Yes. I did." I did not even try to explain.

"I go every six months. Is that what you wanted to know?"

"Yes, that is perfect." I smiled, he shook his head and I rested mine on his shoulder and waited for the music to start again. I snuggled in and smelt his aftershave mixed with his maleness. It was a very comfortable spot to be.

"Christian?"

"Yes?"

"What about allergies?"

"What about allergies?" He asked trying unsuccessfully to mask his annoyance.

"Do you have any?" I persisted.

"I'm developing one to inane, badly timed questions."

We danced to one more song and as I went to open my mouth he said,

"No more questions Julia. What is going on?"

"I realised when we started dancing that it was one of many things we have never done together. There is so much we don't know about one another and I was trying to redress the balance." I explained.

"Okay, so tell me what you now know about me?" He said laughing.

"I know that you love Michael, dogs and the ocean. I know that you are a talented painter and a good dancer who visits the dentist regularly and has no allergies ... and I know that when you touch me I want to be in your bed."

He kissed me there, on the dance floor in full view of the ex-wife and his family and friends and that told me more than any questions I could think to ask.

We arranged to meet for breakfast at the hotel the next morning. I longed to have him beside me tonight but we needed to talk fully clothed and rationally. I needed a pheromone free atmosphere for that.

We tried to talk at breakfast but many of the wedding guests were staying at the hotel and kept coming up to our table to share their reminisces from last night including Rebecca and Jean who wandered off hand in hand to share their love with the greater Paris community.

We walked across the Pont Neuf to the Right Bank and ambled along to the Jardin des Tuileries and Paris continued to work her magic. Not even a non art-loving philistine could fail to be moved by its beauty. The juxtaposition of classical art and modern sculpture shocked initially but the melding was so seamless that you soon accepted as totally normal the sight of a van decorated with a lit crystal chandelier sitting in the classical style fountain in the Tuileries. Children played amongst the giant gumboots and pigeons sat irreverently on the heads of statues of Greek gods and goddesses. I had a momentary flashback to my goddess costume and the photo with Robert. There were absolutely things we had to talk about.

We grabbed a takeaway espresso and perched ourselves on a bench in the gardens and watched tourists emerging from L'Orangerie after seeing Monet's Waterlilies. Their faces universally shared the same look of wonderment and awe.

We sipped our coffees in silence enjoying the sun on our faces and the aroma of the steaming coffee. I started to speak and then stopped – of all the misunderstandings that had occurred between us what was the one thing that still hurt? Did I believe him that Rhonda had stolen his phone and deleted my messages? Yes, I did. Did I care that he slept with her? I cared but not enough for it to matter. The one thing I found hard to understand and forgive was how cruel he had been when he phoned me in New York.

"Did you sleep with Rhonda in retaliation for my supposed date with Robert at the Halloween Ball?" My question cruelly shattered the quiet that had surrounded us.

Christian looked at his feet and the pigeons fossicking for crumbs. I was not sure if he was searching for the right words or debating whether to tell me the truth.

"No. I did not really doubt your honesty but yes, I was jealous." He paused, crushed his paper cup in his fist and moved it from hand to hand like a stress toy.

"I slept with Rhonda the night before I saw the photo, the night before I phoned you."

He looked at me for a reaction and I did not disappoint. Tears welled in my eyes and I said,

"But that makes your accusations and cruelty even less explicable."

"I know and I hated myself even as I was attacking you." He said.

"But why then?" I asked.

"I think I was punishing you for being right. I wanted to punish you for seeing that my Achilles' heel was always giving in to Rhonda. If I could convince myself that you had cheated on me than my behaviour was justifiable." He tossed the crumpled cup into a nearby rubbish bin and even at such a serious moment he could not hide the smile that escaped his lips at his athletic prowess. He turned to face me once more and asked,

"Can you forgive me and can you believe that I have exorcised her hold over me for good?"

I thought of last night and the kiss on the dance floor.

"I forgave you long ago and yes, I do believe you."

"Can I ask you something then Julia?" I nodded. "The guy, in the photo were you attracted to him?"

"Yes, I was but nothing happened. In fact I bored the pants off him talking about you all night." I explained.

"He can't have been too bored Julia if he followed you to Sydney."

"He didn't follow me; he just happened to be transferred to a university in Canberra and he looked me up." I justified.

"I think he did more than look you up didn't he?"

I had the grace to look sheepish and I jumped in before he could ask any more searching questions.

"And yes, before you ask we did date for a while. He was a very decent man but the more time I spent with him the more I missed you. I tried to move on but found that I couldn't." I started to hum *I got you under my skin* and he smiled and that beguiling dimple stabbed me in the heart.

"One more question Julia," Please don't ask if we slept together you can assume it but please don't ask I prayed, "how often do you go to the dentist?"

I felt that I had gone four rounds with Mike Tyson and I'm sure Christian felt the same. We walked back holding hands and one dog after another crossed our path.

"You really miss Max don't you?"

"It's ridiculous but there seems to be this hole in my life when I am at home. I keep expecting to see him bringing me his lead and demanding a walk. He and Michael grew up together. I miss them both."

"You need a change of scene Christian."

"Do I? What did you have in mind? He asked.

31

I FLEW BACK TO Sydney on British Airways. I used the last of my frequent flyer points and upgraded to business class. It was one of those planes where the business seats are configured like sardines in a can, head to toe. There were removable barriers between the seats so it was not compulsory to stare into the eyes of the passenger beside you.

Christian and I had talked and talked and I now knew his favourite movies and books. I knew about his first girlfriend at six and his first kiss at twelve. He had finally given me the painting of Rantua Abang that had featured in the newspaper article. I did not know that it was possible for a man to blush vermillion but he did when I told him about the email that was doing the rounds of cyberspace.

I knew where I was going to hang it. I think subconsciously I had left the space vacant for it even before I knew of its existence. I would be able to sit and look at the waves breaking on the sand in the full glare of an Australian sun and see the gentle moonlight casting its glow over two young lovers at the same time.

I was excited to get back to my gallery. Jess said the repairs were now complete and we had a big exhibition coming up and she needed my eye to choose and hang the works. *Windswept and Interesting* was doing equally well and its structure as a co-operative was a godsend for Christian as it gave him the time to pursue his own painting while still receiving an income.

The seat beside me was still unoccupied but I could see someone walking purposefully towards it. He reached up to place luggage in the overhead locker and as he stretched to open it he showed a satisfying expanse of toned belly. He reached over to push the dividing barrier down that separated the two seats.

“What kept you?” I asked

“If you misbehave I'll put this back up.” He said gesturing towards the divider.

He sat down, reached across and entwined his fingers with mine.

“So,” I said indicating the moveable divider, “that was the last barrier between us then?” I never could resist an obvious pun.

He grimaced, shook his head sadly and said sotto voce,

“And to think that I fell in love with the woman!”

The flight attendant refreshed our champagne and we raised our glasses and I proposed a toast.

“Here's to sun, sand and seascapes and that long overdue Australian holiday.”

“Shouldn't there be another ‘s’ in that list?” He asked as he reached across and licked a dribble of champagne off my lips.

It was going to be a very long flight.

www.ingramcontent.com/pod-product-compliance
Ingram Content Group UK Ltd.
Pitfield, Milton Keynes, MK11 3LW, UK
UKHW020143250726
13967UKWH00002B/829